UNEXPECTED TRANSFORMATION

Sood clutched at the stone, tugging at it so Kincar was dragged forward, the chain cutting into his neck. But that chain did not break, and the stone fell back against Kincar's skin, a blot of searing fire, to cool instantly.

Sood stood still, his hand outstretched, the fingers bent as if they still held the Tie. Then, holding that hand before him, he began to roar with pain and the terror of a wounded beast, for the fingers were shriveled, blackened—it was no longer a human hand.

STAR GATE

A Del Rey Book

BALLANTINE BOOKS • NEW YORK

RLI: $\dfrac{\text{VL: } 7+ \text{ up}}{\text{IL: } 6+ \text{ up}}$

A Del Rey Book
Published by Ballantine Books

ISBN 0-345-31193-0

This edition published by arrangement with Harcourt Brace
Jovanovich, Inc.

Manufactured in the United States of America

First Ballantine Books Edition: December 1983

Cover art by Laurence Schwinger

1

Inheritance

This had been a queer "cold" season so far. No snow, even on the upper reaches of the peaks, no drifts to stopper the high passes, warm winds over the fields of brittle stubble, though most of the silver-green leaves of the copses had been brought to earth by those same winds. Instead of cold they had experienced a general drying-out to kill the vigorous life of wood and pasturage. And the weather was only a part of the strangeness that had settled over Gorth—at least those parts of Gorth where men beat paths—since the Star Lords had withdrawn.

The Star Lords, with their power, had raised the Gorthians above the beasts of the forests and had thrown over them their protection, as the lord of any holding could now extend the certainty of life to one outlawed and running from sword battle. But now that the Star Lords had gone—what would follow for Gorth?

Kincar s'Rud paused beneath the flapping mordskin banner of Styr's Holding to direct a long, measuring glance along the hill line. His cloak, sewn cunningly from strips of soft suard fur brought back from his solitary upland hunts, was molded about him now by the force of that unseasonably warm wind, as he stood exposed on the summit of the watch tower alert to any movement across the blue-earthed fields of the Holding. Kincar was no giant to boast inches rivaling a Star Lord's, but he was well muscled for his years and could and had surpassed his warrior tutors in sword play. Now he absently flexed one of his narrow, six-fingered hands on the rough stone parapet, while the banner crackled its stiff folds over his head.

He had volunteered for this post at midday, for no other reason than to escape the sly prodding of Jord—Jord who affected to believe that the withdrawal of the Star Lords meant a new and brighter day for the men of Gorth. What kind of day? Kincar's eyes—blue-green, set obliquely in his young face—narrowed as he traced that thought to the vague suspicion behind it.

He, Kincar s'Rud, was son of the Hold Daughter and so ruler by blood as soon as Wurd s'Jastard went into the Company of the Three. But if he was not alive to walk this Holding, then Jord would be master here. Through the years since he had been brought from the city to this distant mountain Holding, Kincar had overheard enough, pieced-together bits of information, until he knew what he would have to face when Wurd did depart into the shadows.

Jord had his followers—men whom he had gathered together during his trading journeys—who were tied to him by bonds of personal loyalty and not by clan reckoning. And he appeared able to smell out advantages for himself. Why else had he come down the long trail two days ago, heading a motley caravan? Ostensibly it was to bring the latest news of the Star Lords' departure, but it was strange that Wurd had just taken to his bed in what could only be that ancient man's last bout with the old wound that had been draining his strength for years.

Would Jord attempt to force sword battle on Kincar

for the Holding? His constant oblique remarks had suggested that. Yet outwardly to provoke such a quarrel when Jord himself was the next heir after Kincar was to court outlawing as Jord well knew. And Jord was too shrewd to throw away his future for the mere satisfaction of removing Kincar. There was something else, some other reason beneath Jord's preoccupation with the Lords' withdrawal, behind his comments on the life to come, that made Kincar uneasy. Jord never moved until he was sure of his backing. Now he hardly attempted to veil his triumph.

Kincar could not remember his mother, unless a very dim dream of muted colors, flower scent, and the sound of soft weeping in a shadowed night were to be named Anora, Hold Daughter s'Styr. But he could never reconcile in his mind the fact that Anora and Jord had been brother and sister. And certainly Jord had given him often to believe that whatever lay between them, hate had been its base.

Though he had been born in Terranna, the city of the Star Lords, Kincar had been brought to the Holding when he was so young that he could not remember anything of that journey. Nor had he ever seen the plains beyond the mountain ring again. Now he did not want to. With the Star Lords departed, who would wish to visit the echoing desolation of their city or look upon the empty stretches where their Star ships once stood? It would be walking into the resting place of the long dead who were jealous when their sleep was disturbed.

He did not understand the reason of their going. The aliens had done so much for Gorth—why now did they set off once more in their ships? Oh, he had heard the blasphemous whisperings current among those who followed Jord, that the Star Lords denied to Gorth's natives their great secrets—the life eternal with which they were blessed and the knowledge of strange weapons. He had also heard rumors that among the Lords themselves there had been quarreling, that some had wished to give these gifts to Gorth, while the others chose to withhold them, and that those who would give had gathered a fighting tail of Gorthians to rebel. But since the Lords had withdrawn, what could they now rebel against—the open sky? Perhaps in the hour of their leaving the Lords had set a curse upon this rebellious world.

Though the wind about him continued warm, Kincar shivered. Among his people were those with the inseeing, the power to drive out certain kinds of sickness by the use of hand and will. How much greater must be such powers among the Star Lords! Great enough to lay a spell upon a whole world so that the cold came not? And later would there follow any season of growing things once more? Again he shivered.

"Daughter's Son!"

Kincar had been so occupied with his own imaginings that his hand went to the hilt of his sword as he whirled, shocked alert by that hail, to see Regen's helmed head emerge from the tower trapdoor. But Wurd's guardsman did not climb any farther.

"Daughter's Son, the Styr would have speech with you."

"The Styr—he is—?" But he did not need to complete that question; the answer was to be read plainly in Regen's eyes.

Although Wurd had taken to his bed days ago, Kincar had not really believed that the end was so near. The old chief had ailed before, had been close enough to the Great Forest to hear the sighing of the wind in its branches, yet he had come back to hold Styr in his slender fist. One could not picture the Holding without Wurd.

Kincar paused in the hall outside the door of the

Lord's chamber only long enough to tug off his helm and drop his cape. Then, with his drawn sword gripped by the blade so that he could proffer the hilt to his overlord, he went in.

In spite of the warmth there was a fire on the hearth. Its heat reached the bed on which was piled a heap of coverings woven from fur strips. They made a kind of cocoon about the shrunken figure propped into a sitting position. Wurd's face was blue-white against the dark furs, but his eyes were steady and he was able to raise a claw finger to the sword hilt in greeting.

"Daughter's Son." His voice was only a faint whisper of sound, less alive than his eyes. It died away in a silence as if Wurd must gather and hoard strength to force each word out between his bloodless lips. But he raised again that claw finger in a gesture to Regen, and the guard moved to lift the lid of a chest that had been drawn forward to a new position beside the bed.

Under Wurd's eyes Regen took out three bundles, stripping off coverings to display a short-sleeved shirt of scales fashioned of metal with the iridescent sheen of a reptile's skin, a sheathed sword, and, last of all, a woven surcoat with a device, new to Kincar, worked upon the breast. He thought that he was familiar with Wurd's war gear, having been set to the polishing of it many times in his younger days. But none of these had he ever seen before, though their workmanship was that of an artist in metal, and he thought that their like could not be equaled save perhaps in the armories of the Star Lords.

Shirt, sword, and surcoat were laid across the foot of the bed, and Wurd blinked at them.

"Daughter's Son"—again that wavering claw pointed —"take up your heritage—"

Kincar reached for that wonder of a shirt. But behind his excitement at the gift, he was wary. There was

9

something in Wurd's ceremonious presentation that bothered him.

"I thank you, Styr," he was beginning, a little uncertainly, when that hand waved him impatiently to silence.

"Daughter's Son—take up—your whole heritage—" The words came in painful gasps.

Kincar's grasp of the shirt tightened. Surely that could not mean what he thought! By all the laws of Gorth, he, Hold Daughter's Son, had a greater heritage than a scale shirt, a sword, and a surcoat, fine as these were!

Regen moved, picking up the surcoat, stretching it wide before his eyes so that the device set there in colorful pattern was plain to read. He gasped in amazement—those jagged streaks of bolt lightning with the star set between! Kincar moistened lips suddenly dry. That device—it was—it was—

Wurd's shrunken mouth shaped a shadow smile. "Daughter's Son," he whispered, "Star Lord's son—your inheritance!"

The scale shirt slithered through Kincar's loosened grip to clink on the floor. Stricken, he turned to Regen, hoping for reassurance. But the guard was nodding.

"It is true, Daughter's Son. You are partly of the Star Lords' blood and bone. Not only that, but you must join with their clan—for the word has come to us that the rebels would search out such as you and deal with them in an evil way—"

"Outlawry—?" Kincar could not yet believe in what he heard.

Regen shook his head. "Not outlawry, Daughter's Son. But there is one here within Styr's walls who will do rebel will on you. You must go before Styr is departed, be out of Jord's reach before he becomes Styr—"

"But I am Daughter's Son!"

"Those within these walls have full knowledge of your blood," Regen continued slowly. "And there are some who will follow you in drawing sword if you raise the mord banner. But there are others who want none of the Star blood in this Holding. It may be brother against brother, father against son, should you claim to be Styr."

That was like coming up with bruising force against a wall when one was running a race. Kincar looked to Wurd for support, but the old lord's still bright eyes held the same uncompromising message.

"Where shall I go?" he asked simply. "The Star Lords have left."

"Not—so—" Wurd's whisper came. "Ships have gone—but some remain— You shall join them. Regen—" He waved a finger at the guard and closed his eyes.

The other moved quickly. Almost before he knew what was happening, Kincar felt the man's hands on him, stripping off ring mail, the jerkin under it. He was reclad in the scaled shirt, over it the surcoat with its betraying insignia. Then Regen belted on the new sword.

"Your cloak, Daughter's Son. Now down the inner stair. Cim awaits you in the courtyard."

Wurd spoke for the last time, though he did not again open his eyes, and the words were the merest trickle of sound. "Map—and the Fortune of the Three with you—Daughter's Son! You would have held Styr well—it is a great pity. Go—while I still hold breath in me!"

Before Kincar could protest or take a formal farewell, Regen hurried him from the room and down the private stair to the courtyard. The mount that he had

11

trapped in the autumn drive pens two years previously and knew to be a steady goer, heavy enough for good work in the press of a fight, and with an extra stamina for long travel on thin rations, stood with riding pad strapped about its middle, saddlebags across its broad haunches.

Cim was not a beautiful larng, no sleek-coated, nervous highbred. His narrow head whipped about so all four of the eyes set high in his skull could survey Kincar with his usual brooding measurement. His cold-season wool was growing in patches about the long thin neck and shoulders, its cream-white dabbed with spots of the same rusty red as the hide underneath. No, Cim was no beauty, and he was uncertain of temper, but to Kincar's mind he was the pick of the Holding's mount pens.

But Cim was not the only thing in Styr Hold that he could claim as his own. As Kincar settled on the larng's pad and gathered up the ear reins, he whistled, a single high, lilting note. He was answered from the hatchery on the smaller tower. On ribbed leather wings, supporting a body that was one-third head with gaping, toothed jaws and huge, intelligent red eyes, the mord—a smaller edition of those vicious haunters of the mountain tops, lacking none of their ferocious spirit—circled once over her master's head and then flapped off. Vorken would hover over him for the rest of the day, pursuing her own concerns but alert to his summoning.

"The road to the north—" Regen spoke hurriedly, his hands raised as if he would literally push Kincar out of the courtyard. "The map is in the left bag, Daughter's Son. Take the Mord Claw Pass. We are blessed by the Three that storms have not yet choked it. But you have only a short time—"

"Regen!" Kincar was at last able to break the odd

feeling, which had possessed him during these last few minutes, of being in a dream. "Do you swear by Clan Right that this is a good thing?"

The guard's eyes met his with honesty—honesty and a concern there was no attempt to disguise. "Daughter's Son, by Clan Right, I tell you this is the only way, unless you would go into the Forest dragging half your men after you in blood. Jord is determined to have Styr. Had you been only Daughter's Son, not half of Star blood, none would have followed him. But that is not so. There are those here who will draw blade at your bidding, and there are those who look to Jord. Between you, if you so strive, you will split Styr Holding like a rotten fruit, and the outlaws will eat us up before the coming of green things again. Go claim a greater heritage than Styr, Daughter's Son. It is your right."

For the last time he gave Kincar full salute, and the younger man, realizing that he spoke the truth, set Cim into a lumbering trot with a twitch of the ear reins. But his hurt struck so deep that he did not once turn to look back at the squat half-fortress, half-castle with the cluster of fieldmen's dwellings about its walls.

The wind was at his back as he took the northeast track, which would bring him up to Mord Claw Pass and the way to the interior plains. As far as he knew, he was heading into the broken, aimless life of an outlaw, with the best future he could hope for one in service as a guardsman under some lord who wanted to enlist extra swords for a foray.

Could Wurd's talk of a remaining Star ship—of his joining with the Star Lords—be true? He had half forgotten it since leaving the old man. Kincar fumbled with the left saddlebag and brought out a roll of writing bark. He had been trained to read block characters, for part of his duties at Styr was to keep records. But such reading was not a quick task, and he let Cim pick his own route along the road as he puzzled over the two lines with the small accompanying drawing.

Why—it was clear enough! Those of the half-blood who wished to join the Star Lords had been summoned. And the map was not unfamiliar—it covered a portion of the countryside he had been set to memorize a year or so earlier. Then Wurd had still been able to ride and had carried on the tutelage of the Hold's heir, taking him as far as the passes and pointing out in the wastes below where gatherings of outlaws might exist and where a canny chief of a Holding might well look for future trouble. The map was the heart of such a section, a district of ill omen, rumored to be the abode of the Old Ones, those shapes of darkness driven into foul hiding by the Star Lords upon their arrival in Gorth.

The Star Lords! Kincar's hand went to the device on his surcoat. He had a sudden odd longing to look upon the reflection of his own face in some chamber mirror. Would his new knowledge make any change in what would be pictured there?

To his eyes he had no physical difference from the other youths of Styr. Yet, by all accounts, the Star Lords were giants, their skin not ivory-white as his own but a rich brown, as if they had been hewn from a rare wood. No, if this wild tale were really true, he could have nothing of his sire in face or body. Under his helm his hair curled tight to his skull in small rings of blue-gray. Through the years it would darken to the black of an old man. But it was rumored that the Star Lords also had hair growing upon their bodies—and his skin was smooth. Away from Styr who would know his alien blood? He could discard the surcoat, turn free guardsman—maybe in time raise a following tail and gain a holding of his own by legal sword battle.

But, while he made and discarded half-a-dozen such plans, Kincar continued to ride along the path that would take him over the Mord's Claw and into the wasteland shown on the map. He could not have told why, for something within him shrank from the acceptance of his inheritance. While he revered the Star Lords and had hotly resented Jord's sneers, it was a very different thing to be of off-world blood oneself. And he did not like it.

The day had been half over when he quit Styr. And he did not halt for a rest, knowing that Regen must have fed Cim well. When the track they followed dwindled into a forking trail, he came upon Vorken sitting in the middle of the open space, fanning her wings as she squatted upon the still-warm body of a small wood-suard. He was heading into a country where game might be scarce, and wood-suard was tender eating. Kincar dismounted, cleaned the beast with his hunting knife, giving Vorken the tidbits she hungered for, and slung the body up behind his pad. It would do for the last meal of the day.

Their way up was a winding one. It was a caravan track, only used in times of war when the more western routes were preyed upon by guardsmen. And he was sure that it had not been traveled this season at all— the wastes beyond having too ill a name.

When the slope grew too steep, he dismounted, letting Cim pick a path where the mount's clawed feet found good hold. He scrambled along through scrub brush, which caught at his cloak or the crest of fringed mord skin on his helm. And he knew he was lucky that the season was so warm he did not have to fight snow as well, though here the nip of the wind was keen. Vorken took to hovering closer, alighting now and then on some rock a little ahead of her companions' slow advance to whistle her plaintive call and be reassured by Kincar's answer. A mord, once trained to man's friendship, had a craving for his presence, which kept

15

it tractable even in the wilds where it could easily elude any hunter.

It was close to sunset when the vegetation, dried and leafless, was all behind them and they were among the rocks near to the pass. Kincar looked back for the first time. It was easy, far too easy, in the clear air, to sight Styr Holding. But—he caught a quick breath as he saw that the banner was gone from the watchtower! Wurd had been right—the lordship had passed from one hand to the next this day. Wurd s'Jastard was no longer Styr. And for Kincar s'Rud there could be no return now. Jord was in command—Jord s'Wurd was now Styr!

2

The Battle of the Waste

An overhang of rock gave Kincar shelter for the night. He had crossed the highest point of Mord Claw Pass and come down a short distance to the beginning of the timber line before the daylight faded. But he had no wish to push on into the wilderness beyond during the dark hours. Though the mountain shut off some of the wind, it was far colder here than in the valley of the Holding, and he set about building a traveler's small fire in the lee of the rocks while Vorken settled down upon the pad he had stripped from Cim and watched him intently, spreading her wings uneasily now and again as she listened to sounds from the stunted bushes and trees below them.

With Vorken's ears at his service, and Cim's alertness to other animals, Kincar needed to do no sentry duty. Neither would leave the fireside, and either or both would give him swift warning of danger. He was in more peril from wandering outlaws than he could be from any animal or flying thing. The giant sa-mords of the heights were not night hunters, and any suard large enough to provide a real threat would be timid of fire.

He cut up the meat Vorken had provided, sharpening a stick on which to impale chunks for roasting.

And in the saddlebags he found the hard journey cakes of wayfarers, which packed into their stone solidity enough nourishment to keep a man going for days through a foodless wilderness. Regen was an old campaigner, and now that Kincar had time to check the contents of the bags, he appreciated the thought and experience that had gone into their packing. Food in the most concentrated forms known to men who hunted or raided through waste country, a fishing line with hooks, a darg blanket folded small, its wet-repelling surface ample protection against all but the worst storms, a set of small tools for the righting of riding gear and armor, and, last of all, a small packet wound with a fastening of tough skin that Kincar tackled with interest. Judging by the care with which it had been wrapped, he was sure it must contain some treasure, but when the object was at last bared to view in the firelight, Kincar was puzzled. He was sure he had never seen it before—an oval stone, dull green, smoothed as though by countless years of water action rather than by the tools of men. But there was a hole in the narrower end, and through this hung a chain of metal. Plainly it was intended to be worn.

Tentatively Kincar shook it loose from the hide covering and cupped it in his palm. A moment later he almost dropped it, for as it lay upon his flesh, its dullness took on a faint glow, and it grew warm as though it held a life of its own. Kincar sucked in his breath and his fingers tightened over it in a jealous fist.

"Lor, Loi, Lys," he whispered reverently, and it seemed to him that with every speaking of one of the Names, the stone he held pulsed warmly.

But how had Regen—or was this a lost heritage from Wurd? No one within Styr Hold had ever dreamed that a Tie had lain in its lord's keeping. Kincar was overwhelmed by this last evidence of Wurd's trust in him.

Jord might have the Holding, but not the guardianship of a Tie. That was his! The trust—and perhaps some-day— He stared bemused at the fire. Someday—if he were worthy—if he proved to be the one Wurd hoped he might be, he might even use its power! With a child's wondering eyes, Kincar studied the stone, trying to imagine the marvel of that. No man could do so until the hour when the power moved him. It was enough that a Tie was his to guard.

With shaking fingers he got the chain about his throat, installed the stone safely against his skin under coarse shirt, jerkin, and scale armor. But it seemed that some measure of heat still clung to the hand that had held it. And when he raised his fingers to look at them more closely, he was aware of a faint, spicy fra-grance. Vorken gave one of her chirps and shot forth her huge head, drawing her toothed beak across his palm, and Cim's head bobbed down as if the larng, too, was drawn by the enchantment of the Tie.

It was a very great honor to be a guardian, but it was also dangerous. The Tie could weave two kinds of magic, one for and one against mankind. And there were those who would readily plant a sword point in him to gain what he wore now—if it was suspected to be in his possession. Regen had given him aid and dan-ger tied together in one small stone, but Kincar ac-cepted it gladly.

Without worry, knowing that he could depend upon Vorken for a warning, he curled up with cloak and blanket about him to sleep away the hours of the dark. And when he roused from a confused dream, it was to a soft chittering beside his ear. Vorken was a warm weight on his chest. Outlined against the coals of the dying fire, he saw the black blot of her head turn from side to side. When he moved and she knew he was truly awake, Vorken scuttled away, using the tearing claws

19

of her four feet to scramble to the top of a rock—making ready to launch into the air if need be. Her form of defense was always a slashing attack aimed at the head and eyes of the enemy.

Kincar felt for his sword hilt as she stared into the dark. There was no sound from Cim, which meant that Vorken's more acute hearing had given them time to prepare. What she warned against might well be far down the mountainside. The fire was almost dead, and Kincar made no effort to feed it into new life. His senses, trained during long wilderness hunts, told him that dawn was not far off.

He did not try to go out of the pocket in which they had camped. Vorken still gave soft warnings from her post. But, since her night sight was excellent, and she had not taken to the air, Kincar was certain the intruder that had disturbed her was coming no nearer. The sky was gray. He could pick out the boulders sheltering them. Now he set about padding Cim, lashing on saddlebags, though he did not mount as they edged out of the hollow. Voken took to the air on scout. Cim's claws scraped on the rocks, but within a few feet the trail began and they walked in thick dust. Kincar chewed on a mouthful of journeycake, giving the major portion of the round to Cim. That must do to break their fast until they were sure they were safe.

The trail came out after a steep descent upon the lip of an even more abrupt drop. But Kincar did not move on. Crouching there, he brought Cim up with a sharp tug at the ear reins, hoping that neither had been sighted by the party below.

His first thought—that he spied upon a traders' caravan—was disproved in his second survey of the camp. There were six larngs, all riding stock—no burden bearers among them. And there were six riders on the bank of the small ice-bordered stream. The larngs bore the marks of hard going, their flanks were flat to the bones, and their cold-season wool hung in draggled patches as if they had been forced through thorn thickets.

But Kincar was astonished by the riders, for three of the figures seated on the bank were women, one hardly more than a child. Women in the wastelands! Of course the outlaws raided the holdings and took women to build up their clans. But these were plainly not captives, and their traveling cloaks were fine garments of tetee wool such as Hold Daughters had. They were on good terms with the men, and their light voices were pitched as if they spoke at ease with clan brothers.

What was such a party doing here? They were not out for a day's hunting, for each larng bore traveling bags, plump to seam-bursting. Kincar longed to see their faces, but each wore the conventional travel mask under a well-wound turban of veil. For a moment he had a wild suspicion— This was the waste where the Star Lords had ordered their people to assemble. But there was no mistaking the pale skin of the nearest warrior. He was of Gorthian breed, no being from outer space.

As Kincar hesitated, uncertain as to whether he should hail the others, there was a startling scream from Vorken and then the deep, braying roar of a hand drum.

Those below were on their feet as if jerked up by ropes laid about them. The women, tossed by their escorts unto the riding pads of the waiting larngs, galloped off, one man with them, while the other two warriors reined in their mounts with one hand, holding swords free with the other. There was the sound of a running larng, and a war mount burst out of a screen of brush. Kincar, already up on Cim, paused to stare at the newcomer.

21

His larng was a giant of that breed—it had to be— for the man who bestrode him was also a giant. His wide shoulders were covered with a silvery stuff that drew light even in the gray of early morning. Both of the waiting warriors rode over to take a stand beside him, all three wheeling to await some attack.

Kincar found the zigzag trail down the cliffside. Recklessly he did not dismount but kept the larng to the best speed possible, as loose stones and gravel rolled under Cim's scrabbling claws. The path took one of its sudden turns, and he caught sight of a battle raging in that river clearing.

Men in the tatters and rusty mail of outlaws, some on foot, a few riding gaunt larngs, leaped out of the brush, a wave to engulf the three who waited. But those three met the wave with licking blades. There was a confused shouting, the scream of a dying man. Cim's forefeet were on the last turn and Kincar leaned forward, whistling into his mount's ear that particular call that sent the larng into the proper battle rage.

They burst through the stream in a spatter of high-dashed water, were up the opposite bank and racing toward the melee. Vorken, seeing that Kincar was on the move, planed down to stab at an unsuspecting face, sending the man rolling screaming on the ground as her bill and claws got home. Cim, as he had been schooled, reared, using his forefeet on the dismounted men, while Kincar clung to the riding pad with one hand and swung his sword to good purpose with the other. There were a few wild minutes, and then the roar of the hand drum once again. A man at whom Kincar had aimed a stabbing thrust broke and ran for shelter into the brush. And when Kincar looked about for another enemy, he found that, except for the bodies on the ground and the three men who had been attacked, the pocket meadow was clear.

One of the warriors dismounted to wipe his blade on the grass before sending it home in its sheath.

"Those scouts have now had their fangs drawn, Lord Dillan—"

The man who had just sheathed his sword laughed, a harsh sound lacking mirth. He speedily contradicted his fellow.

"For the moment only, Jonathal. Were they of the common breed one such lesson would suffice. But these have a leader who will not let us away in peace as long as blades can be raised against us."

The giant in the silver clothing looked beyond his own men to study Kincar, a frown line showing between his brows, though little else was to be seen of his features because of the traveling mask across cheek and chin. Something in that close scrutiny brought Kincar's head up. A thrill of defiance ran through him.

"Who are you?" The question was shot at him as quick as a sword stab and as sharply.

"Kincar s'Rud," he replied, with none of the ceremonious embellishment he should use by forms of holding courtesy.

"—s'Rud—" the other repeated, but his tongue gave an odd twist to the name so that it came out with an intonation Kincar had never heard before. "And your sign?" he pressed.

Kincar had tossed aside his cloak. He twisted a little on the riding pad so that the other could see the device worked so boldly on his surcoat—that device that even yet did not seem right for him to wear.

"—s'Rud—" the giant said again. "And your mother?"

"Anora, Hold Daughter of Styr."

All three of them were staring at him now, the warriors appraisingly. However, he must have satisfied the big man, for now the lord held his hand, palm empty, over his head in the conventional salute of friendship.

23

"Welcome to our road, Kincar s'Rud. You, too, have come at the summoning?"

But Kincar was still wary. "I seek a place in the waste—"

The strange lord nodded. "As do we. And, since the time grows very short, we must ride in haste. We are now hunted men on Gorth."

They might be satisfied with his identification, but he had had none from them. "I ride with—?" Kincar prompted.

The silver-clad lord answered. "I am Dillan, and these are Jonathal s'Kinston and Vulth s'Marc. We are all wearers of the lightning flash and followers of strange stars."

His own kind, the mixed blood. Kincar studied them curiously. The two guardsmen, at first glance, seemed no different from well-born holding men. And, though they showed Lord Dillan a certain deference, it was that of clansman to close kin and not underling to hold chief.

The physical difference between Lord Dillan and the others was so marked that the longer Cim picked his way behind the leader's mount, the more Kincar came to suspect that he now rode in company with no half-blood but with one of the fabulous Star Lords in person. His great height, the very timbre of his voice, betrayed an alien origin, even though his helm and face mask and the tight silver clothing concealed most of his body and features. Yet neither Jonathal nor Vulth acted as if their leader was semidivine. They displayed none of the awe that kept Kincar silent and a little apart. Perhaps they had lived all their lives in the shadow of the Star-born and knew no wonder at their powers. Yet in the battle the Lord Dillan had not slain his enemies with shooting bolts of fire, as legend said he might do, but used a blade, longer and heavier than the usual to be sure, but still a sword much the same as that now girded to Kincar's own belt. And when he spoke, it was of common things, the endurance of a larng, the coming of full day, matters that any man riding in company might comment upon.

Vorken whistled her warning from above their heads, and all of them glanced aloft to where she skimmed, wings stretched, gliding on the unseen currents.

"You are well served, Kincar," the Lord Dillan addressed him for the first time since they had left the meadow. "That is a fine mord."

"Aye, a battle bird of price!" Vulth chimed in. "She is quick with her beak where there is need. Of your training?" he ended politely.

Kincar warmed. "I picked her from the egg. She has had two years of coursing. The best of Styr's hatchery for five seasons at least."

Those whose presence Vorken's scream had heralded now came into view ahead. The three women on their weary larngs, their escort trailing a length behind with an eye to the rear. He flung up his arm in welcome at the sight of their party and pulled aside to wait, but the women took no heed, keeping on at the best pace their larngs would rise to.

"You have drawn teeth?" the warrior hailed them.

"We have drawn teeth," Vulth replied with grim satisfaction. "They will press us again, but there are now fewer to answer the drum."

As if his words had been a signal, again that ominous roll of sound struck their ears from the back trail. But it was muffled by distance. The hunters had dropped well behind their quarry. Lord Dillan pushed his mount ahead to fall in with the women. They exchanged words in a low voice, and one of the women pointed in a westwardly direction. The Star Lord nodded and brought his larng to one side, letting the women pass. With a wave of his hand he sent their guard pounding in their wake, while the remaining four slackened speed once more—to provide a rear guard.

Kincar saw with woodswise eyes that they were following a marked trail that had been in recent use, its dust churned by larng claws in ragged lines. Lord Dillan must have noted his examination, for he said, "We are the last of the in-gathering. We have come from Gnarth."

From half the continent away! No wonder their mounts showed bones through thin flesh and the women rode with the droop of weariness in their cloaked shoulders. But certainly they had not been hunted along all that distance? To underscore that thought, the hunt drum rolled again—this time closer. Vorken sounded her war call, but when Kincar did not wheel to face the enemy, she circled over their heads in widening curves, spiraling up into the new day, her keen eyes on the ground, her attention ready for any move from Kincar that would send her once more in a vicious dive against his foes.

The clumps of leafless brush that had narrowed their path since they left the river banks dwindled into patches of small twisted scrub, arid as dried bones in the now waterless land. And the blue earth under foot was pied with patches of silver sand. They were plainly heading into one of the true deserts of the waste. Yet the spoor of those before them was plain to read, and those with whom Kincar now rode appeared certain of the route.

A sun arose, bringing with it the sickly, warmish wind that was so out of season. And, with the wind, the sand came in thin clouds to plague them. Kincar improvised a mask. He was inured to the usual wind grit that bothered city dwellers traveling, but this was something else. Cim closed two of his eyes and veiled the others with his transparent inner eyelids but showed no other signs of discomfort as he trotted along. Vorken soared above the worst of the eddies.

Outcrops of rock, carved by wind and the tempest-borne sand grains into weird sculptures, rose along the trail, as if they were the ruins of some long-sacked holding. And the track wound about among these pillars and towers until Kincar found himself losing his sense of direction, the more so since he could not pick landmarks ahead through the quick flurries of wind and sand.

He was reduced to following Lord Dillan blindly, and only confidence in that leader kept him in control of a growing uneasiness. He was hungry, and water—the thought of water—was a minor torture. They must have been traveling for hours. How much longer would they shuffle on across this barren waste?

Kincar dragged on the reins, forcing Cim to rear up. The roll of the drum had sounded in his very ear! Yet Vorken had given no warning! Then he heard Vulth's voice, muffled by the mask.

"It is the echo, youngling! They stamp yet far behind us—not now have they outflanked our path. But loose your blade in its sheath; it will drink again before sundown—if we find us a proper battleground."

3

No Ship—But—

The weird echoes of the drum made Kincar edgy. To
have it blast from one side and then the other grated
on his nerves, and he longed to draw his sword and
ride with the blade bared across his knee, ready for
attack. But those with whom he rode made no such
preparations, and he was ashamed so to betray his own
uneasiness.

At the same time he speculated concerning their
goal. A sky ship berthed here? Among all the rumors
that dealt with the secrets of the wastelands, there had
never been one that hinted at such a thing. Those ships
at which all of Gorth had marveled had been in the
great landing place outside the gates of the now for-
saken Terranna. And they were gone, through the pale
rose of Gorth's sky, never to return. Had one ship been
set here, apart from its kind? When, from time to time,
there came short breaks in the force of the grit storm,
Kincar held his head high, trying to catch a glimpse
of the shaft of metal of a sky ship, which would dwarf
all about it.

But, though they bored steadily into the desert land,
using the track winding among the pillars, there was
no sign—save that same faint road—that man had ever
gone that way before. The pillars were growing fewer,

and, now that they did not hem in the road, there was the danger of going astray in the fog of wind-driven sand. Lord Dillan slackened pace, sometimes halting altogether for a moment or two, one hand close to his chest, his head bent over it, as if he consulted a talisman. And after each such move he altered their course to the right or left.

Then, as quickly as it had arisen, the wind died, the sand lay once more in dust-fine drifts, and the land about them was clear to the view. They were on an upslope, and far ahead Kincar sighted moving dots of figures, which must be the women and their guard. Those bobbed to the skyline and then were suddenly gone. They might have been sucked down in the sand. A downgrade lay beyond, Kincar surmised, and a steep one or they would not have vanished so quickly.

Jonathal brought his larng up beside Cim, wiping the matted dust from his mouth mask with the back of his hand before he commented thickly, "That was a dry course! And I've never relished a fight without a cold draft to sweeten the throat—"

"A fight?" Kincar had not heard the drum for a time. He had hoped that the storm had shaken their pursuers from the trail.

"They must attack now." Jonathal shrugged. "This is the last throw of tablets in the game. Once we are over that ridge"—he jerked a thumb at the rise—"they will have lost. We are the last of our kind. With us through, the gate will close—"

Kincar did not understand that reference to the gate, but he understood very well the scream from Vorken's long throat, her skimming dive that carried her black shadow back over the sand dunes toward the pillar-studded land from which they had just emerged. And now, at last, he drew his sword, rolling his cloak about his left arm as a shield, ready to snap it into an opponent's face if the need arose.

Figures slipped from pillar to pillar, silent, dark, misshapen. Kincar watched that sly, noiseless advance, set his mouth hard. For five years or more he had ridden in holding spear-festings aimed against outlaws, and once he had served in a real foray against Crom's Hold. In the last two festings, in spite of his youth, he had taken out Styr's banner as Wurd's deputy. He had known such warfare since his small boy's hand had first been fitted to an even smaller sword hilt under Regen's patient teaching. But this was something else—he was sensitive to a change, wary under a threat he did not understand.

Vorken wheeled back above him, shrilling her battle cry, but not attacking since he had not advanced. Cim shifted foot under him. They must feel it, too, this difference, this odd threat that promised worse than slash of sword, thrust of footman's spear, clash of mounted man against his kind.

His sword dangling from his wrist cord, Kincar brought up his right hand to jerk off his dust mask, drawing in more freely the air for which his lungs felt a sudden need. Jonathal was on his left, sitting at ease on the pad of his gaunt larng, a smile curving his mouth as he watched the pillars with a sentry's eye. On the right Vulth was making a careful business of adjusting his cloak about his arm, testing each fold as he laid it ready. But Lord Dillan, his one hand laced in larng reins, his other still held to his breast, had not drawn his weapon at all or shed his travel mask. Above the strip of silver stuff that matched his garments, his odd light eyes were on the pillars and what moved in their shadows.

"Ride slowly," he bade them. "We do not fight unless they push us to it—"

"They will not let us away out of their jaws," warned Vulth.

"Perhaps they will—unless he who leads them gives

the order—" Lord Dillan did not relax his watchfulness or turn his larng after them as the other three followed his orders and headed on.

Kincar was last, reluctant to leave. And at that moment Vorken went into action on her own. Whether the mord misconstrued Cim's movement as an advance, or whether her natural wildness sent her in, Kincar was never to know. But she gave vent to one last whistle and snapped down in a glide toward the nearest pillar.

He did not see the bolt that caught her in mid-air. No one could have sighted the silent, swift stroke. But, as Vorken shrieked in pain, one of her wings collapsed, and she hurtled down toward the sand. Without pausing to think, Kincar sent Cim skimming back to where Vorken lay, beating her good wing in a vain attempt to win aloft again. Her cries were growing hoarser in her pain and rage, and she was hurling spurts of sand into the air with her four feet as she dug fruitlessly with her claws.

Kincar was off Cim. He hit the ground already running, his cloak whipping out to net the frenzied mord. To take her up barehanded was to court deep tears from claws and beak. Somehow he scooped up cloak and struggling creature, cradling her tight against his chest while she snapped and kicked in fury.

There was a shout of triumph from the pillars; a shaggy wave came out of hiding, heading straight for Kincar. He retreated, watchful. His sword was ready, but Vorken's struggles hampered its free use. He was facing spear points, clubs, in the hands of lithe-moving footmen, and in that moment he realized that the uneasiness he knew was truly fear. The openness of their attack was so removed from their usual methods of battle that it alarmed him as much as the stench from their unwashed bodies made his empty stomach churn.

He gave the cry to summon Cim. But, though the larng obediently trotted to his side, Kincar could not scramble up on the pad, not with the still-fighting Vorken pressed against him. Yet he would not abandon the mord.

"Yaaaaah—" The shout of the outlaws echoed about him in a worse tumult than the beat of the drum. And behind the footmen, better clad and armed, mounted men were joining in the rush to ride him down.

Then a larng dashed between him and that advance, the sand fountaining about mount and rider. Vulth thrust and raised a dripping blade for a second stroke. More men boiled from the pillars to get at them both.

With the fraction of breathing space, Kincar had gotten up on Cim, his sword banging from its wrist cord. He let the reins hang. The larng was well enough trained to need no guidance during a fight. The mount was snarling, pawing at the sand, and he reared when he felt Kincar's weight on the pad, clawing down one of the spearmen.

Vorken must be half stifled. She had ceased to struggle, and Kincur was grateful for that as he fell to such sword work as would cut a path for Vulth's withdrawal.

A voice shouted incomprehensible words. Lord Dillan replied in the same tongue with a single bitten-off sentence. His blade was out, and he rode beside Jonathal as if they were the two arms of a single warrior. The outlaws broke, snarling like the beasts they were, and ran, but the mounted men behind them were of a different breed. Jonathal's larng snorted and spun around despite the efforts of its rider to control it. Then it fell with the slack-legged force of an already dead animal and Jonathal was crushed under it, only the soft sand saving him from mortal injury.

Kincar brought Cim up to split the skull of the bare-headed outlaw who had his point at Jonathal's throat as the other fought to pull free of the larng. Then, above the hum of the drum and the cries of the fighting men, there struck a peel as shrill as Vorken's calls. Up over the rise, toward which they had been headed, boiled a group of riders. There were only five of them when Kincar could at last sort them out, but somehow the fury of their charge magnified their numbers into double that score.

They swept past the four, scooping up the outlaws and bearing them along by the force with which they struck into the melee. But they did not pursue past the line of the pillars, wheeling there so shortly as to make their larngs rear and totter on their hind legs. Then they pounded back. One paused to let Jonathal scramble up behind him before they went on, drawing the others with them, over the ridge and down into a deep cup of valley, a bare valley that lay like a giant pockmark in the desert waste.

As they swept across the crest, Kincar reeled, his knees almost losing their grip on the riding pad. The sensation of bursting through an unseen barrier was part of that shock. But with it, and worse, had come a thrill of white-hot pain. So sure was he that some chance-thrown spear had found its target in his body that he stared stupidly down to where he still clasped the muffled Vorken, expecting to see metal protruding from his breast and wondering vaguely how he had survived a blow of such force. But there was no spear point showing, and, as he straightened again, he knew that he had not been hit. Only—what of that stab of agony, the pulse of heat and pain that he still knew beneath scale coat and underjerkin?

The Tie! For some reason beyond his knowing, its unique properties had been aroused in that second when he had topped the ridge. The why of it he could not guess, and he dared ask no questions. Those who were guardian of a Tie in the Name of the Three held

34

that honor secretly, a secrecy accepted without complaint as one accepted the other burdens and rights such a duty laid upon one. He did not dare to touch the space above his heart where that throb beat as if in promise of worse to come.

In the heart of the valley was a camp—a hasty affair of small shelters put together with blankets and cloaks. These were now being speedily dismantled, men throwing rolls and bundles on the backs of larngs. Beyond the camp stood something else, as different from the primitive shelters as one of the Star ships might be from a trader's wain.

Two pillars of bright blue metal had been based in piles of rocks, the supporting stones being fused into a stability no storm could shake. They were erected some five feet apart, and suspended between them was a shimmering web of some stuff Kincar could not name. It was bright; it glittered with racing lines of rainbow fire that ran ceaselessly crisscross over it—yet it had so little real body that one could see through it to the opposite wall of the valley.

Kincar shifted Vorken's weight upon his arm and regarded this new marvel intently. He had come here expecting to discover a Star ship. He had found a web strung between metal poles. What had his trust in his chance-met companions drawn him into? As far as he could see, they were now trapped. The outlaws need only make one last rush to wipe them out—for there were no more than six men waiting here.

Of those six, four were wearing the silver dress of Lord Dillan, and they were of the same giant stature. They had put off their travelers' masks, and he could see the alien darkness of their hard faces, the features of which lacked the mobility of those he had known all his life. One of them now raised his hand in a salute, which Lord Dillan answered. Then that other lord took in his big hands the leading lines of three of the waiting larngs and moved toward the shimmering web. As they watched, he stepped between the supporting pillars.

There was no discernible break in the web. For a moment the rainbow lines rushed in to outline the figure of the Star Lord—then those colors fled again to the far corners of the screen. But the Star Lord and the larngs he had led—were gone! They did not reappear on the opposite side, and Kincar blinked at the wavy sight of the rocks beyond where no one—no thing—walked at all!

Vorken gave a faint chirrup in his arms; the tip of her beak pushed forth from the wrappings that netted her. Cim blew noisily, clearing the sand grit from his wide nostrils. But at that moment Kincar could neither have spoken nor moved.

It would appear that the tales of the Star Lords' magic, the wildest tales of all—at which sensible men had laughed indulgently—were true! He had just seen a Star Lord walk into nothingness, which perhaps a Star Lord might safely do—but what of the rest of them?

" 'Tis the gate, youngling!" Vulth's knee brushed against Kincar's as the other rode beside him. "The gate to give us a new world."

The explanation meant exactly nothing to Kincar. A ship that went out to the stars—aye, that could he understand. He was no ignorant fieldman to believe that the sky over one's head was merely the great Shield of Lor held up between men and a terrible outer darkness without end. And he knew well that the Star Lords had come from another world much like Gorth. But they had come in ships where a man could live, the fabric of which all curious ones could feel with their two hands. How could one seek another world by walking through a veil of shimmering stuff?

His hand flattened over the Tie and his lips moved in the Three Names of Power. This was a magic that the Star Lords had not—a magic native to Gorth. And at this moment it was far better to cling to such a talisman than trust to a veil that took men out of sight in an instant.

It was apparent that Vulth knew what to expect and that this wonder was no magic in his eyes. Cim picked his way through the draggle of tents in the wake of Vulth's mount, but Kincar neither urged him on nor tried to restrain him. Now one of the half-bloods had taken the lead ropes of two more laden larngs. And, as had the Star Lord before him, he went forward with the confidence of one walking a city street into the web where the colors haloed him for an instant of flaming glory before he vanished, the animals after him.

Then it was that Vulth turned and caught Cim's dangling reins. He smiled reassuringly at Kincar.

"This is a venture better than any foray—past even the Foray of Hlaf's Dun, youngling. Past even sky voyaging—"

Kincar, clutching Vorken with one hand, the other resting above the branding heat of the Tie, made no protest when the warrior sent his larng straight on toward the screen gateway. He was aware only dimly of sharp glances from Star Lords who stood nearby, for his full attention was on the web. He could not throw aside the thought that he was about to be engulfed in a trap of some kind beyond his imagining. He braced his body stiffly against the inward shrinking of his nerves, against the impulse that would have sent him pounding away not only from the gate but from those who controlled such a device.

Vulth vanished into nothingness; Cim's head was gone. Kincar was drowning in a sea of color. And on his breast the Tie burned with a force that seemed to char through flesh to his heart. He bit back a whimper of pain and opened dazzled eyes upon a world of gray stone—a world in which life itself seemed alien, intruding, a world of—no, not the dead, for there had never been life here at all—but a world that had never known the impress of a living thing. How he sensed that, Kincar could not have told—perhaps such knowledge came through the Tie.

He straightened painfully, conscious of a party crowded on the stretch of rock plain. But he did not see Vulth's eyes upon him, the odd shadow on the older Gorthian's face as he witnessed Kincar's obvious distress. Nor did Kincar follow when the other dropped Cim's reins and rode on to join the group waiting by a second portal a half mile farther on.

There was a second portal—the same blue metal poles supporting another rainbow web. Only, before this one was a box contrivance where the Star Lords were clustered. One of their number knelt before that box, his hands resting upon it, a tenseness in his position arguing that he was engaged in some act of the utmost importance.

Cim wandered along, his head drooping. Kincar drew a slow and painful breath. The hurt of the Tie had eased a little. Only when he was directly in touch with the Star Lords' magic was it so great an agony. If they were to pass through another such gate, could he stand it? He tried to fix his thoughts upon the Three. The Tie was Theirs, the right to bear it had been set upon him by Them—surely They would aid Their servant now—

He tried to watch those about him, gain some hint of what this was that they must do. There were women here, laden supply larngs, a full caravan of travelers. But in all, the party numbered less than thirty, and

38

only six of those in sight were Star Lords—all the rest must be of the half-blood strain.

There was clearly clan feeling among them, the easy meeting of kinsman with kinsman. Only he felt set apart, torn from all he had known. If only he could know what was happening, where these gates led, what lay before them now! Of one thing he was growing increasingly sure—they were headed into an exile that would be permanent.

A Star Lord burst through the first gate. He ran toward his fellows. Those gathered by the box looked up, their faces strained and bleak. If he bore a warning, they had too little time to act upon it, for through the first gate poured a jumble of mounts and men, swinging bloody steel, and two of them rode double.

The Star Lord at the box moved his hand, bringing down his palm with a smacking force. There was a ripple of green on the second web; the hue became blue, then purple-red as it moved.

Lord Dillan reeled through the first gate. Only two steps beyond it, he staggered about and brought up his hand. What he held Kincar could not see, but from his fist there sprang a spear of light that burned bright in the gloom of that gray world. It struck full upon the first web. The stuff curled, wrinkled, and was consumed as a cobweb fallen into a flame. Between the posts one could see only the barren rocks.

But those who had waited here were now in a hurry to be gone, as if the destruction of that one web was not enough to save them from their enemies. Kincar was caught up in line, and he dared not protest, setting his power of endurance to meet what might chance at his second passage through the magic gates.

It came as an agony worse and deeper than either of the earlier two attacks. He thought he must have cried out, but no one near him took note—perhaps they were too intent upon escape. He was conscious that the sky above was no longer gray but a familiar rose, that Cim's feet crackled through dried field grass. And Vorken stirred in his arm, crying peevishly.

He looked about him dazedly. This was not the wasteland. He saw a roll of wide plain, the rounded mounts of foothills in the distance, and above, the loom of mountains. A chill wind puffed into his face, bringing with it icy particles of snow, and more white flakes were swirling down in an ever thickening fall.

4

New-Found World

Kincar shivered. Dare he free Vorken from her wrappings in order to bring the cloak about them both? Injured and frightened as she was, the mord might well rend him—for there was a vast, sinewy power in the small body he pressed so tightly against his own. And the burning torment on his breast had sucked from him both strength and inclination to struggle.

So intent was Kincar upon his own problem that the growing clamor about him meant very little. He gathered, only half-consciously, that the Star Lords had been forced by a sudden attack on the outer gateway into action that might prove highly dangerous. And there was a dispute that ended only with the destruction of the second gate, the one that had brought them into this range of open, rolling land. For better or worse, they were now committed to this place, wherever it might be.

Kincar hunched over Vorken, squeaking to her softly in his closest imitation of her own voicings, cautiously loosening the cloak. To his great relief she did not respond with an instant thrust of stiff legs armed with dagger talons. And when he dared to drag the folds entirely away, she crouched, staring up at him, almost as if her fierce nature had for once been cowed by the events of the past hours. She reached out with her forefeet and took firm hold on the breast of his surcoat as she might cling to the bare bole of some tree she had selected for a roost.

Kincar shrugged the cloak about them both, though his movements were slow because of the trickles of pain that ran from the Tie across his shoulders and along the nerves of his arms. It was good that he need not draw sword now. He doubted if he could raise the weight of the blade.

But he did examine Vorken's injured wing, finding across its leathery surface a finger-breath of raw brand, a burn. She allowed him only a moment's inspection and then turned her head and licked at the hurt with her tongue, meeting his further attempt at examination with a warning hiss. And he was forced to allow her to tend her hurt in her own way, only glad that she was content to ride under his cloak without protest.

The Star Lords were marshaling them into line. This open country in a gathering snowstorm was no place for a camp, and they were heading through the swirls toward the foothills where some form of shelter could be expected. To Kincar's eyes the country was oddly deserted. This was too good crop land not to be included in some holding—yet there was no sign of wall, no view of field fort, as far as he could see. By some magic the Star Lords must have brought them into a section of Gorth where there were no holds at all. He was very certain they *were* on Gorth. The sky above them was pale rose, the grass, dried in clumps and edging out of the already covering snow in ragged bunches, was that he had always known. Aye, this was somewhere on Gorth—but where?

At a shout he brought Cim into the line of march. There were no familiar faces near him. And he was too tired, too plagued by the Tie, to try to seek out Jonathal, or Vulth, too shy to look for Lord Dillan in that company.

Luckily the snow did not take on the proportions of a blizzard. Tired, hungry, cold as they were, they could keep one another in sight. But there was little talk along that line. They rode with the suppressed eagerness of those who have been long hunted and who now seek a sanctuary, intent upon winning to such a goal. As the foothills came into clearer view, a pair of scouts broke from the main party and galloped ahead, separating to search the higher ground in two directions.

Cim was only plodding. He had not eaten since they had left the pass camp—had that only been this morning? He must be allowed rest, food, and that very soon. Kincar was debating a withdrawal out of line, to give the larng some journeycake, when one of the scouts came pounding back at a dead run. The excited gabble of his report was loud, though his words were not clear. Some sort of superior shelter had been located—it was ready for them. And, as if to underline their need for just such as that, the wind moaned across the empty land and brought with it a thicker flurry of snow, while heavy clouds scudded in the sky. A blizzard was not far off.

The wind might be a broom the way they were swept by it into a narrow valley. But the gloom of the dying day could not hide—hide or belittle—what awaited them there. Kincar had seen many marvels since he had ridden out of Styr. And this was not the least of them.

Here was a hold such as a lord of limitless acres might dream of building. Its square towers bit into the reaches of the sky; its walls had the same solidity as the gorge rock in which it was set. And it spanned the narrow valley from side to side, as if, massive as it was, it served as gate as well as fortress.

In the hollow of a doorway—a doorway so wide that at least three burden larngs might enter it abreast—stood one of the Star Lords, in his hands a core of yellow-red light blazing as a beacon to draw them on through the murk of the snow. But above, in that dark bulk of tower and wall, there was no other light—only shadows and a brooding silence, which seized upon and swallowed up the muted sounds of their own progress down the valley. Kincar knew that this fortress was a dead, long-deserted pile.

As it was deserted, so was it subtly different from the hold forts he had known, not only because of its size, but also because of some alterations of line. Those who had erected this had not first practiced on the building of such as Styr—they had had other models. Then Kincar thought he understood. This was some hidden hold of the Star Lord. It probably guarded the field on which their last ship stood. He knew that their city of Terranna had been far different from the native holds. And that business of the gates had yet to be made clear. But this then was the goal toward which they had headed. He slid down from Cim, cradling Vorken in his arm. Under him the ground was unsteady, and he was forced to snatch at the riding pad with his other hand to keep his balance.

Still holding to Cim, Kincar went on slowly until the doorway arched above him and he was in a passage lighted by one of the Star Lords' flares. There was no side opening in that passage, and it brought him into a courtyard, ringed in with hold walls, into which some snow was shifting down—though the major part of the storm was kept off by those same walls. Here two more flares showed a stall section under a roof, a structure that could only be a mount pen, and Kincar, through habit, headed for it.

Perhaps it was the effect of the Tie that made him

move as if in a foggy dream. Mechanically he went through duties that had been drilled into him in childhood, but his sense of curiosity and his awareness of others about him were oddly dulled. It might have been that only Cim, Vorken, and he were alive in that place.

Cim entered one of the stalls readily enough. There was no blanketing hay for its flooring, and Kincar's boots grated on stone flagstones. As he loosened his cloak, Vorken struggled free of his grip and fluttered her good wing, sputtering her distress, until he lifted her to where she could cling to the top of a stall division, a poor substitute for her roost in the hatchery, but it appeared to satisfy her for the present.

Then he stripped Cim of pad and bags. With an undershirt from his scant wardrobe, he began to rub down the snow-wet flanks, press the excess moisture from shoulder and neck wool, until Cim bubbled contentedly. But with every movement of his hands and arms Kincar's fatigue grew so that he was obliged to lean for long moments against the wall of the stall panting. He kept doggedly to his task, ending by feeding the larng crumbled journeycake in his cupped hands and holding up to Vorken a strip of dried meat from his provisions.

Cim folded long legs in the curiously awkward stance of a larng needing rest. And the coarse crumbs of journeycake were still on Kincar's tongue as he fell rather than lay down beside the mount. He reached for his cloak and pulled it up, and then he remembered nothing at all—for a dream world engulfed him utterly and he was finally lost in a darkness without visible end.

Pain—dull and not biting as he had known it—still centered on his breast. Kincar tried to raise his hand to ease it, and a sharper nip caught one of his fingers, completely arousing him. A toothed bill above his chin, red eyes staring into his, a whistling complaint—Vorken crouched on him. His head rested on one of Cim's forelegs, and the heat of the larng's body kept him warm. But his breath puffed a frosty cloud in the air.

Someone must have closed the door of the stall pens. He was looking now at ancient wood, eaten by insects, splintered by time—but still stout enough to be a portal. Vorken, having seen him fully awake, walked down his body and, trailing her hurt wing, crossed to sit on the bags, and demanded to be fed from their contents.

Some of that strange fog that had dulled his mind since he had dared the web gates had been lost in slumber, but Kincar still moved stiffly as he stretched and went to answer the mord's demands.

Though the outer door of the building was in poor condition, as trails of snow shifting under it and through its cracks testified, the structure itself was in as good repair as if it had been hewn from the mountainside. He marveled at those huge blocks of stone that made up the outer walls, laid so truly one upon the other that the cracks at their joining were hardly visible. The lord who had raised this hold must have been able to command master workers in stone, or else this was more of the Star Lords' unending magic. For all Gorth knew, those from off-world could command the elements and tame the winds, if it was to their desire. Terranna had been a marvel. The only point that puzzled Kincar now was the aura of age that clung to this fortress.

Of course Gorthian time was a matter of little moment to the Star Lords with their almost eternal life. They could die in battle right enough, or from some illness. But otherwise they did not show signs of age until their years had equaled five, even six life spans of the natives—three hundred years was not unknown for men who in that time displayed no outer marks of age at all. And among them before the withdrawal there had still been some who had landed on Gorth almost five hundred years earlier.

But, though they had such a length-of-life span, they did not produce many sons or daughters to follow them. That had been first whispered and then said boldly abroad. And when they took Gorthian mates, the issue of such marriages were also few—two children to a marriage at the most. So their numbers had remained nearly the same as when they had first landed their sky ships, a limited number of births balancing deaths by battle or misadventure.

If they were responsible for the building of this hold, it must have been erected soon after they reached Gorth, Kincar was certain of that. This type of stone exposed to the open air darkened with the passage of time. But he could not remember, save in the scattered stones of a very old shrine, such discoloration as these walls displayed. Yet history had never placed the Star Lords far from their initial landing point of Terranna. And where was this?

His thoughts were interrupted by Vorken's demand, which arose from a hissed whisper to ear-punishing squawks, punctuated by the flapping of her good wing. As he went down on his knees to burrow in the bag that contained his food, the door to the courtyard opened with a protesting scrape, letting in a blast of frigid air and a measure of daylight.

There was a chorus of grunts and sniffles from the larngs in the line of stalls, impatient for feeding and watering. Both men who entered carried buckets slopping over at their brims. In spite of Vorken's protests Kincar got to his feet. And the first man uttered a surprised exclamation as he caught sight of the young man—just as Kincar himself was mildly astonished to see that the other was one of the silver-clad Star Lords setting about a pen task normally left to a fieldman, and no concern of a swordwearer.

"And who are you?"

"Kincar s'Rud." Vorken, completely losing her temper, snapped at his hand, and he tossed her a meat stick from the bag.

"And soon to be an icicle by the look of you," commented the Star Lord. "Did you spend the night here?"

Kincar could not understand his surprise. Of course he had spent the night with Cim. Where else did a warrior sleep on the trail but with his larng? The stone was hard, aye, but a warrior did not notice such discomfort—he must be prepared to accept as a matter of course far worse.

The half-Gorthian with the Star Lord set down his two buckets and chuckled. "Lord Bardon, he but follows custom. In enemy territory one does not separate willingly from one's mount. Is that not so, youngling? But this is not enemy territory now. Tend to your beast and then in with you to the hall. There is no need to freeze in the line of duty." Then he added with the bluff good humor of a captain of guardsmen to a new recruit, "I am Lorpor s'Jax, and this is the Lord Bardon out of Hamil."

Hamil—another far distant district in the west. Indeed this in-gathering had caught up those from odd corners of the world. Having fed Vorken, Kincar fell to and helped the others care for the line of larngs. The animals, used to sparse feeding during the cold months, were given slightly larger rations of journeycake because of their recent hard usage. But most of them were already settling into the half-doze that carried them through the short days of snow-time, unless their services were needed. Cim's upper eyes were fast closed when Kincar returned to his stall to collect bags and

Vorken, and his lower ones regarded his master with a dull lack of interest.

Vorken allowed herself to be picked up, but scrambled out of his arm to cling to his shoulder, balancing there a little uncertainly, her injured wing trailing down his back. Lorpor inspected the burn on the leathery skin and whistled softly.

"Best show her to the Lady Asgar—she has healing knowledge. Perhaps she can cure that so this one may fly again. A good mord—of your own training?"

"Aye. From the shell. She was the best of the hatchery at Styr."

Lorpor had fallen into step with him as they crossed the snow-drifted courtyard toward the middle portion of the hold. And now Lord Bardon shortened pace so that they caught up with him.

"You came in with Dillan?" he asked Kincar abruptly.

"Aye, Lord. But I was not of his following. I am from Styr Hold in the mountains—" Kincar volunteered no more information. He found Lord Bardon's sharpness disconcerting—hinting that he had no right to be there. Yet Lord Dillan had received him readily, so perhaps this brusqueness of speech was peculiar to Lord Bardon. Never having been among those of the pure Star blood, Kincar could only watch, listen, and try to adapt to their customs. But he felt no ease in their presence as did the other half-bloods such as Jonathal, Vulth, and Lorpor. In fact, that ease of manner between them and the Star Lords in turn made him oddly wary of them. And for the first time he wondered about his father. Why had he, Kincar, been sent away from Terranna, back to Styr, when still a baby?

True, it was the custom that Hold Daughter's Son lived where he was heir. But neither was such a boy kept so great a stranger to his father's clan and kindred. Kincar had always thought of his father as dead—but— His boot sole slipped on a patch of snow, and Vorken hissed a warning in his ear. What if his father still lived? What if he was to be found among the lords of this company? For some reason Kincar, at that moment, would rather have faced a ring of swords barehanded than ask information concerning the "Rud" whose name he had always borne.

"Styr Holding—" Lord Bardon repeated that as though trying to recall some memory. "And your mother was—?"

"Anora, Hold Daughter," Kincar returned shortly. Let this Lord know that he was not of the common sort.

"Hold Daughter's Son!" If that had not registered with Lord Bardon, it did with Lorpor. His glance at Kincar held puzzlement. "Yet—"

"Being half-blood," Kincar explained against his will, "I could not raise Styr Banner. There was Jord s'Wurd, Hold Daughter's brother, to dispute."

Lorpor nodded. "With the trouble hot about us, that would be true. And to set brother fighting brother is an evil thing. You did well to seek out another future, Hold Daughter's Son."

But Lord Bardon made no comment, merely lengthened his pace and was gone. Lorpor drew Kincar through a doorway into a hold hall that was twice the size of any he had ever seen. Huge fireplaces at either end gave a measure of heat, not from any pile of well-seasoned logs, but from small boxes set on their hearths to radiate warmth—some more Star magic. Riding pads were stacked to furnish seats, huddles of traveling bags and cloaks marked the occupancy of individuals or families, and there was a babble of sound through which the deeper voices of the Star Lords made an underthread of far-off thunder.

"Leave your bags here"—Lorpor pointed to a place on the pads—"and bring your mord to the Lady Asgar."

Kincar shed his cloak in the heat of the chamber before Lorpor guided him out of the main room of the hold into a side chamber, which jutted out like a small circular cell. The half-blood halted at a cloak hung curtainwise and called.

"Lorpor, with one who has need of healing skill, my lady."

"Let him enter and speedily," came the answer, and Kincar stepped through to face a woman.

She wore the short divided skirt of a traveler, but she had put aside all head and shoulder wrappings, except for a gold and green shawl caught over her plain green bodice. It was her face that startled Kincar close to forgetting all manners, for this was the first Star Lady he had ever seen.

In place of the long braids of a Gorthian woman, her hair was cropped almost as short as his own, and it lay in waves of gold as bright as the threads of her shawl, doubly bright about the creamy brown of her skin. The eyes she turned toward him were very dark, under level brows, and Kincar could not have guessed at her age, except that he did not believe her to be a young maid.

She saw at once the purpose of Kincar's visit and held out her hands to Vorken, giving a chirruping cry. Knowing the mord's usual response to any touch, Kincar tried to ward her off. But Vorken surprised him by climbing down along his arm and reaching her long neck, her hideous head, to those brown hands.

"Do not fear, boy." The Lady Asgar smiled at him. "She will not savage me. What is her name?"

"Vorken."

"Ah—for the Demon of the Heights! Doubtless it suits her. Come, Vorken, let us see to this hurt of yours."

The mord gave a short leap, beating her good wing, to the lady's grasp.

She carried the mord over to the full light of the

window, examining the drooping wing without laying hand upon it.

"A blaster burn. But luckily only the edge of the ray caught. It can be restored—"

She held Vorken close to the wall, and the mord, as if obeying some unspoken order, caught at hollows in the stone with all four of her feet, clinging there while the Lady Asgar went to some bags and brought forth a tube of metal. This she pointed at Vorken's hurt and held it so for a long second.

What she did or why Kincar did not know. What he was acutely conscious of was the Tie, again awakened to angry life against his flesh. And, perhaps because this was the fourth time he had known such torment, he reeled back against the wall, unknowing that his face was a haggard mask, that Lorpor was watching him with a surprise close to horror. Only dimly did he feel an arm flung about his shoulders, was only half aware of being brought back against a sturdy support that kept him on his feet, while the Lady Asgar spun around, her astonishment altering to deep concern.

5

A Question of Birthright

Only for a moment did Kincar remain so steadied, and then, the stab of the Tie less, he pulled away, glancing up to see that it was Lord Dillan whose hands still rested on his shoulders. The rigid brown mask, which, to his untutored eyes, served all the Star Lords for a face, had a new expression. And Dillan's voice, when he spoke, was warm with concern.

"What is it, Kincar?"

But the young man freed himself with a last twist and stood, one hand at the breast of his scaled shirt, schooling his body, his nerves under control. He who carried a Tie was honored above his fellows, as well as burdened, but his guardianship was not for the knowledge of others—certainly not for the outland-born Star men. So he fronted all three of them with the same wariness with which he would face a company of strangers in a time of clan feud when enemy was not yet sorted from friend.

When he made no answer, Lord Dillan spoke to the woman.

"What happened?" He used the common speech, purposely, Kincar suspected. Kincar himself wanted nothing more than to be out of that room and away from their prying eyes.

"I used the atomar on the mord—it has a ray-burned wing."

"The atomar," Lord Dillan repeated, his attention once more fixed on Kincar, as if by his will he could force the truth from the young man.

"He fears the Star machines—" That was a new-comer speaking, and there was contempt in his voice. Vulth stood in the door, eying Kincar as he would some wood creature brought in by a hunter. "It was so that he flinched upon passing the gates—as well I saw. Doubtless at his hold they held to the old belief in night demons and howling terrors—"

Kincar was ready with a hot retort to that, but he did not give it voice. A good enough explanation for his behavior if they had to have one, one that made him less of a man, that was true, but it was better to shrink in the regard of these (though that in its way carried a hurt also) than to reveal what he carried.

A brown hand closed about the wrist of his sword hand, keeping him where he was, and the Lady Asgar was beside him. Something in her manner must have relayed an order to both Vulth and Lorpor, for, after glancing from her now impassive face to that of the Lord Dillan, they went out, Vulth unhooking the up-turned corner of the cloak door and letting it fall to give the remaining three privacy.

Kincar tried to follow, but that hand still gripped his wrist. Short of forcibly twisting free, he could not leave. But when the Lady Asgar spoke, he lost his desire to do so.

"The Tie of the Three is a heavy weight for the bearing—"

His hand flattened convulsively against that weight. Mechanically he gave the proper response.

"To the bearer it is no weight, it is a lightener of

54

loads, a shortener of ways, a brightener of both day and night."

Now her hand dropped away. "So did I think!" Swiftly her fingers sketched a certain sign between them in the air, and he stared at her wonderingly.

"But"—that was half protest, half unbelief—"you are wholly of the Star Blood. You do not tread the Road of the Three!"

"To each race there are certain beliefs granted." She spoke as she would to a child under instruction. "We, too, have our powers—though they may not take the same form for our worshiping. But all who follow Powers of Light give faith and belief where it should be. I, who am counted as a wise woman among my people, share in part the learning of the Three. Could I give you these signs were that not so?" Again she cut the air with brown fingers—those ten fingers so alien to his own twelve. "But, Kincar, this you must know for your own protection. Some forces which we bend to our use can in turn make a Tie serve as a transmitter, should one be within the range of their influence. And the greater the volume of that force, the greater its focus upon the Tie. To cross the web—" She shook her head. "You must bear wounds now as deep as if a sword had struck you down. Those must be treated before evil comes of them."

"As you treated Vorken?"

She shook her head. "That force would only add to your torment. The healing of Gorth, not the healing of Star lore, must be brought to your flesh. But that healing is also mine. Will you suffer my tending?"

He could accept her knowledge; she had given him good proof of what she knew. But Lord Dillan? She might be reading his thoughts, for now she smiled and said, "Did you not know that Lord Dillan is also a healer—of our clan? Though his healing reaches out into twisted minds instead of serving lamed bodies. He has taken the Inner Path, been a disciple of the Forest, with the Seven Feasts and the Six Fasts behind him these many years."

"I was a man of Gormal s'Varn." Lord Dillan spoke for the first time. "Though that is indeed now many years behind us—"

Gormal s'Varn! The leader on the Path who had lived many years before Wurd's grandmother! Again that oppressive feeling of the past that clung to these walls and was also a part of the Star people lapped about him. But in that moment he surrendered his will to the two, given confidence by their learning.

It was the Lord Dillan who aided him with the buckles of his scale shirt, helped him draw off the jerkin and soft shirt under it, while the Lady brought out from her bags small jars, two of which she opened, spreading a rich fragrance of dried summer flowers and grasses in the cold, too ancient air of the place.

The Tie swung free, but at the point where it had been cradled tight to his flesh, there was a deep scored mark of angry red, a brand of burning as deep as if white-hot metal had been held there to his torment.

The Lady Asgar produced a skeleton of leaf, which lay like a cobweb across her palm. On this with infinite care she spread creams from her pots, first dipping from one and then the other, blending the oils into the wisp of thing she held, working with the care of an artist applying the last touches of color to some masterpiece. Vorken climbed down the wall and crawled to her feet. The mord's head swayed to and fro on her long neck as she savored the scents that came from the pots. And now and again she gave a beseeching chirrup.

Lady Asgar laughed at the mord's excitement. "Not

for you, winged one." But the mord continued to crouch before her with hungry eyes upraised.

The web-leaf with its healing salves was applied to Kincar's breast, adhering there as tightly as if it were another layer of skin. But neither Lord Dillan nor the Lady touched the Tie. But she studied it carefully and asked, "Are you a Looker, Kincar?"

He made haste to deny any such power. "I am nothing, Lady, save Kincar s'Rud, who was once Hold Daughter's Son to Styr and am now a landless man. This came to me from Wurd who was Styr. And it came secretly. I found it among my gear when I was quit of the Holding. I have no power of its bestowing, and I think that Wurd gave it me because by right I was Styr and only ill chance took my inheritance—"

But Lord Dillan shook his head slowly, and Kincar could read the dissent on the Lady's more expressive face.

"A Tie does not pass by chance, Kincar, you know that. If Styr was a guardian, then his was the need to select the one who came later, and the man he chose would not be fitted by birth or kinship, but by what lay within him. Also the Tie is always given secretly, lest evilly disposed ones intercept it and corrupt its use to their own purposes. You may not yet have the powers, but who can say that you will not—"

It was the Lady who interrupted. She stood rubbing her finger tips slowly together and so dispensing a flowery scent to the cold room. "The Tie is of the Gorth we know. I wonder whether it will function in this Gorth also—"

Kincar had picked up his swordbelt. The plaster had not only soothed the burn, he was feeling more vigorous than he had since he had passed through the web gates. "The Gorth we know—this Gorth—" Those two phrases

57

rang oddly. As he hooked the belt about him, he puzzled over their meaning.

"This is Gorth?" he ventured.

And he was relieved when Lord Dillan nodded. But then the Star-born continued bewilderingly, "This is Gorth, but not the Gorth into which you were born, Kincar. Nor is it the Gorth we would have chosen to enter. It is a Gorth strange to us and one in which we are friendless and alone."

"You mean—by your magic, Lord, we have been transported over the bitter water seas to the far side of the world?"

The Lady Asgar sat down on one of the riding pads, and straightway the mord climbed into her lap. She sat there, allowing Vorken to nuzzle her scented hands, and now and then stroking the mord's grotesque head.

"We have been transported, aye, Kincar. But not across the seas. Explain to him, Dillan, for as he joined us so late, he will know nothing of what we have done, and we must all face what comes to us with understanding."

"It is this way." Unconsciously Lord Dillan began with the phrase of a song-smith, but his frowning seriousness said that this was no account of fancy. "When it came time that we must go out of Gorth—"

There Kincar found the courage to ask a question that had puzzled him since the news of the Star Lords' withdrawal had come to Styr. "But, why, Lord, was it necessary for you to go from Gorth? Aye, men of ill will have raised their voices. But we never heard such talk until the Lords first said they were going. You have brought the people of Gorth up from forest-dwelling barbarians. Why do you leave them without the shield of your protection when you have so much to give them? Your magic—could it not be shared?"

Again both of them shook their heads. "Instead of

being a protection to Gorth, we may have been its bane, Kincar. When a man-child stumbles about the hall, still unsteady on his feet, do you set in his baby hands a war sword and leave him to his own devices? Or, worse still, do you give him such a weapon and strive to teach him how to use it before his thoughts are formed to know good from ill? In our own world we are an old, old people with a long and dusty trail of years between us and the beginnings of our history. We are the warriors of mature years, though still with many failings in judgment, and in Gorth we have put sharp swords into the hands of little children. We thought we were aiding Gorth to a better life wherein man could have many things he had not. So we taught and wrought with our hands and spread out the fruits of our learning for the plucking of those who wished. But, as children, they were attracted by the hard bright things, the metal which could be forged into blades, the mind-turning which could set one man against another. Had we not landed upon Gorth, had we not meddled, perhaps it would be a happier world, a greater world—"

"Or there could have remained just beasts," Kincar said.

"That is an argument-answer which has come readily these past years," the Lady Asgar answered. "But it is a too ready one. And we have it on our hearts that we may have guided children's feet into false paths. Aie, sadness, sadness—" The words of her own tongue came from her, slow and heavy as tears, and Lord Dillan took up the tale once more.

"So there grew three groups among us. There were those who said that, though it was very late, perhaps even now if we withdrew from Gorth the memory of us, the skills we had taught, would gradually become overlaid by time in the minds of men, and that Gorth

59

could build a world of her own—twisted by some of the gifts we had so rashly given—but still returning to her own heritage, re-fashioned in a way native to her. Then there were those, luckily a very few, who were of a different mind. There will always be born, in every race and species of man, Kincar, certain individuals who have a thirst for power. To them an alien race, should it not be as advanced as they, exists only to serve them. Among us these few were not satisfied with things as they were, but for a different reason.

"They desired full rulership over Gorth, wanted the men of Gorth as servants and slaves. And secretly they began to circulate stories among those landless men, the outlaws, who were willing to form a fighting tail for any lord who would bring them much loot and rich living. Those of them that we could, we brought to justice secretly." His mouth was a thin line and the force of his will was almost a tangible thing as he spoke. "Thus they pushed us into hurried decisions. The major portion of our company voted to take to the ships, to go out once more into space seeking another world, one where there was no native race we might corrupt by contact. But—"

And here the Lady broke in as if this section of the tale was more closely hers.

"But there were others of us, Kincar, who, though we were not of mixed blood, had taken Gorth to our hearts. And when we came to think of raising from her, we could not bear it. So we sought another path of flight. And two men who had been working for many years—lifetimes—on a problem in research thought that they had the solution. It is a difficult one to explain, but it offered us a way to leave the Gorth of troubles for another Gorth in which we might live as we wished. And we labored to turn their theory into fact. This you must tell of, Dillan, since you were one of those men." She smiled at the Star Lord.

He squatted on his heels, and with his forefinger drew lines on the dusty floor as he talked.

"This has been a thoery among our people for a very long time, but until this past year there has been no proof of it in fact. To explain it— Well, Kincar, think upon this. Are there not times in a man's life when he has a decision to make which is of major importance in shaping his future? You had the choice of joining with us, or of remaining at Styr to fight for your rights. Thus, at that moment before you rode from that Hold, you had two roads—two separate futures—and probably very different ones."

Kincar murmured assent.

"Then this is true, as we have proven. There now exist two different Gorths for you—one in which you stand here with us, one in which you held to Styr."

"But how could that be?" Kincar's protest was quick. "I stand here—I do not battle against Jord in Styr—or lie dead from his sword!"

"This 'you' stands here—the other 'you' is in Styr."

Kincar blinked, distrusting this new thought. Multiple "yous"—or "I's"—all acting separately, leading different lives? How could Kincar s'Rud be so split? Once more the Lady Asgar came to his rescue.

"The Kincar who chose to remain in Styr," she said softly, "would not be the Kincar who came through the gates in our company, for, by his very decision, he made himself a different person in a different world. He is not you, nor have you now any part in him—for that world is gone."

Lord Dillan studied the lines he had drawn. "But as it is with men, so it is also with nations and with worlds. There are times when they come to points of separation, and from those points their future takes two roads. And thus, Kincar, there are many Gorths, each formed by some decision of history, lying as these bands, one beside the other, but each following its own path—"

Kincar stared down at those faint marks. Many Gorths, existing one beside the other but each stemming from some crossroads in the past? His imagination caught fire, though still he could not quite believe.

"Then," he said slowly, trying to find the right words, "there is a Gorth into which the Star Lords never came, in which the wild men of the forest still live as do the animals? And perhaps a Gorth from which the Star Lords chose not to withdraw?"

Lord Dillan smiled; he had an eager look. "That is so. Also there are Gorths—or at least one Gorth, we hope—in which the native race never came into being at all. It is that Gorth we sought when we came through the gates."

"But which we were not given the time to find," Lady Asgar murmured. "This fortress proves that."

"Had we not been hunted there at the end, had we had but a day—or maybe only an hour more—we might have found it. Still, with the knowledge we have brought with us, we can open the gates once again—just give us a fraction of time."

But even Kincar was able to sense that behind those brave words Lord Dillan was not so sure. And he asked a question.

"Where are we now? Who built this fort? It is not of any fashion that I know. I thought it to be a hidden hold of the Star Lords."

"No, it is none of ours. But it will give us good shelter for a necessary space. Had we only been granted more time—!"

"At least"—Lady Asgar put Vorken gently on the floor and got to her feet—"your destruction of the gates brought one advantage. If it did not serve us very well, it served Gorth—since Herk came to his end in that blast."

Lord Dillan sat back. "Aye, Herk is safely dead. And those he gathered as a following will quickly melt away, their own jealousies and passions driving them apart. He was the last of the rebels, so Gorth is now free to seek its own destiny, while we may seek ours in another direction."

He stood up, and now he smiled at Kincar with a warmth and true welcome. "We are but a handful, yet this is our venture and we shall have the proving of it to the end. Let us seek out the materials we need and we shall have a new gate with time enough to choose which world it will open to us."

"Lord!" Vulth relooped the door curtain. "The gate box has been reassembled—"

"So!" Dillan was away without farewells, but the Lady Asgar put out a hand to stop Kincar when he would have gone after.

"It is not so easy." She was grave. Behind her serenity she was considering some problem. "The time before we can build another gate may be a long one."

"In Gorth—the old Gorth," Kincar commented, "the Lords had all the magic supplies of Terranna to aid them in such a building. They have been forced to destroy some of that. Can they find such magic here?"

She stood very still. "You bear with you that which must give you ever the clear sight. Aye, that is the stone within our fruit—perhaps for us a gate may not rise again. Dillan will try to rebuild, for that is his life. But his efforts may come to nothing. I would know more of this Gorth—for our own protection I would know. How far back in time was the turning which cleaved our Gorth from this one? Who built this hold and why did they forsake it? Are we in a world emptied

63

by disaster—or one only too well peopled? That we must learn—and speedily."

He thought he could guess at what she hinted. "I have not the Sight," he reminded her.

"Nay. But you are closer to Gorth than those of full Star blood. And you wear that which may bind you closer still. If the Sight comes to you, do not deny it, speak aloud—to me or to Lord Dillan. It is in my mind that Herk forced a bad choice upon us and ill shall come here. See, I have not the Sight, either, yet foreboding grows upon one. And you?"

Kincar shook his head. He could not pretend to a sensitivity he did not have, and, privately, neither wanted nor thought he would ever develop. So far the only effect that the Tie had had on him was physical. He could play guardian, but he was willing to relinquish even that task when the time came that he could pass the talisman to one of the proper temperament to make full use of its powers. Wurd had never been a farseer nor seer, yet he had held the Tie in his time. Guardianship did not always accompany use.

He marveled at the tale he had heard of worlds beside worlds. But he had no premonitions and he wanted none. He would give thanks for his healing, for Vorken's, but he was not ready to join forces with the Lady Asgar in that way. And she must have guessed that, for she smiled wearily and did not try to detain him longer.

6

Legend Come Alive

The gale was brisk, but there was no more snow, and the wind had scoured away the early fall, save where the powdery stuff clung in pockets between trees and rocks. Vorken swung on a high branch, her large head seeming to shake disparagingly above the surrounding countryside as she kept watch. If any creature stirred there, she would mark its path.

Kincar leaned against the bole of the large tree, surveying the domain that their fortress guarded. It was indeed a holding of which any great lord could well be proud. Beyond the narrow neck of the entrance valley, which the hold spanned from wall to wall—an efficient cork to front any enemy—the land opened out into a vast valley ringed about with heights. There might be passes over those mountains, trails out of the valley that did not pass the hold, but so far the newcomers had not discovered them. And all indications pointed to the assumption that the valley of the hold was the only practical entry into the open ground beyond.

From this distance up one of the flanking mountainsides, one could trace the boundaries of old fields, see the straggle of tree stumps, fallen branches, and a few still sturdy trunks marking an orchard. Aye, it had been a rich land, well able to provide a rich living for the hold—once.

But now no harvests from those fields or orchards lay—except as powdery dust—in the storerooms of the fortress. Men must hunt, prowling the wooded slopes of the heights in search of game. So far the results had been disappointing. Oh, now and again one would chance upon a suard or some forest fowl. But they were thin, poor creatures.

This was the first day Kincar had deemed Vorken healed enough to take afield, and he was pinning his hopes upon her aid in a profitable hunt. But, though she had soared and searched in her usual manner, she had sighted nothing. And her rests, during which she clung to some roost well out of his reach, muttering peevishly to herself, grew longer and closer together. The mord might turn sullen with such constant disappointment and refuse to go on unless some success came soon.

With a forlorn hope of flushing a wild fowl, Kincar started ahead, thrusting through any promising stretch of shelter brush. A few scratches and a more intimate, and unwelcome, acquaintance with local vegetation was his only reward. However, he kept to the task.

He heard the stream before he found it—the tinkle of free running water. Then he saw, rising from the narrow cutting in the hillside, misty white tails that might be breath puffed from a giant's lungs.

To his surprise there was no edging of ice on the shore line, and it was from the surface of the water those smoky lines rose. Intent upon the phenomenon, he cautiously slid down the steep slope. There was a disagreeable smell, as well as steam, about him—a strong, acrid odor that made his eyes water as a warm puff drove into his face, setting him coughing. Very warily Kincar put out an investigating finger. The water was not clear, but a reddish-brown, and it was hot enough to sting. He raised the wet finger to his nose and sniffed a fetid smell he could not give name to.

Eager to see from where it sprang, he traced back along the cut until he found the place where the discolored water bubbled out of the mountain's crust. Yet that was not a spring, but a round hole, water worn and stained red-brown, an exit from some depths beyond. Kincar could perceive no immediate use for his find, but, in spite of the odor, the warmth of the water was welcome in the chill, and he lingered, holding hands ill-protected by their clumsy wrappings into the steam.

He was watching the brown swirls of the water, without close attention, loathe to climb back into the cold, when an object bobbed to the surface of the oily flood, struck against a stone, and would have been swept on had Kincar not grabbed for it. He snapped out a pair of pungent words as he scooped it out, for here the water was far hotter than it had been downstream. But he held the prize safely—the thing that had come out of the mountain.

It had begun as a chip of wood, buoyant and fresh enough to possess still the pale yellow color of newly cut zemdol. But it was no longer just a chip. Someone had used it for idle shaping such as he had often seen a man do in Styr, to try out a new knife, or for the pleasure of working with his hands through dull hours in the cold season. The chip now had the rough but unmistakable likeness of a suard. There were the curling horns worn in the warm seasons, lost in the cold, the powerful back legs, the slender, delicate forefeet— a suard carved by one who not only had an artist's skill in his fingers but a good knowledge of suards!

Yet it had bobbed out of the heart of the mountain!

And it was not of the fugitives' making, that he was sure of. Where had the builders of the fortress retreated—underground? Kincar was on his feet, searching the wall of rock and earth from which the stream bubbled, striving to see on its surface some indication that there was an entrance here, that someone who was a hunter of suards and had tried out his knife upon a fresh chip of zemdol had a dwelling therein.

They had all puzzled over the history of the hold. There had been no signs that it had been stormed and sacked, no visible remains of those who had reared its massive walls for their protection, tilled the fields beyond. And the Star Lords said that such a place could not have been taken easily, not even by the weapons of which they alone possessed the secret. They were inclined to believe that some plague had struck down the valley dwellers without warning. Except of that there was no evidence either. All the rooms, from nooks in the watchtowers to eerie hollows hacked out of the rock under those same towers' foundations, probably intended for dark purposes the present explorers did not care to imagine, were bare of anything save dust. If the people of the valley had gone to plague tombs, they had carefully taken with them all their material possessions.

Kincar turned the chip over. This was evidence of other life in the mountain land, though he could not be sure how far from its source the water had carried it. But he was inclined to believe that the temperature of the flood, far higher here than it was downstream, suggested a beginning not too far inside the mountain. And it might be at that birth spring that the carver had lost his work.

The desire in Kincar to get to the root of the mystery was strong. But no one was going to move those tons of earth and rock. So at last, having put the chip in his belt pouch, he climbed out of the cut, which held the hot stream, into the frostiness of the upper air, where the wind bit doubly sharp because of his respite in the warmth.

He whistled to Vorken, and her answer came from farther down the slope. As he worked his way along, he saw her take to the air again in an ascending spiral, and he brought out the weapon Lord Dillan had entrusted to him, to be used only if they were sure of a kill. One held the tube balanced—so—and pressed the forefinger on a stud. Then ensued a death that was noiseless, an unseen ray that killed, leaving no mark at all upon the body of the slain. Kincar did not like it; to him it was evil when compared to the honest weight of sword or spear. But in a time when a kill meant food—or life—it was best.

Vorken no longer cried, her circles for altitude were bringing her up level with the peaks. Plainly she was in sight of her quarry. Kincar waited where he was to mark her swoop—there was too good a chance of warning the prey if he went on right now.

The mord brought her wings together with a snap he could hear plainly through the dry, cold air. Now she was at strike, her four feet with claws well extended beneath her as she came, air hissing from her open bill. There was a high scream as she vanished behind tree-tops, and Kincar ran.

He heard the beat of thumping feet through the brush and crouched. A suard, its eyes wide with terror, burst between two saplings, and Kincar used the strange weapon as he had been instructed. The animal crumpled in upon itself in midleap, its try at escape ending in a roll against a bush. Kincar ran up—there were no claw marks on it. This could not have been Vorken's prey. Had they had the excellent good luck of finding a small party of the animals? Sometimes the suard, usually solitary creatures, banded together, especially in a section where there was poor feeding. Rudimentary intelligence had taught the animals that concentrated strength brought down small trees whose bark proved cold season food.

Kincar paused only to bleed the suard he had killed, and then he sped on—to discover his guess had been right. A tree, its roots dug about, had been pushed to the ground and a goodly part of the tender upper bark shredded away. A second suard lay on the scene of the feast, Vorken's claws hooked in its deep fur. She welcomed Kincar with a scream, demanding to be fed, to have the part of the kill rightfully hers. He set about the gory task of butchering.

The suard Vorken had brought down was prepared for packing back to the hold and the mord was eating greedily before Kincar moved to the other kill. As a trained hunter he walked silently to the place where the second body lay—so silently that he surprised another at work. As he caught sight of the figure hunched above the suard on the bloodied snow, saw those hands busy at the same task he had just performed, he froze. This was no partner from the hold. Unless one of the children had slipped away to trail him—

Then the other turned to strip back a flap of furred hide. This was not a child in spite of the small body, the hands half the size of his own, which worked with the quick sureness of long experience. The face beneath the overhang of the fur hood was that of a man in his late youth, a broad face bearing the lines of bleak living. But when the stranger got to his feet to walk about the suard, his head could not have reached a finger width above Kincar's shoulder. As he himself was to the Star Lords, so was this one to him. The compact body, muffled as it was with furs and thick clothing, showed no signs of malformation—the manikin was well proportioned and carried himself as might a trained warrior.

But had the other been as tall as Lord Dillan himself, Kincar would have jumped him now. To see this dwarfish creature calmly about the business of butchering the suard he had killed, preempting meat so badly needed in the hold, was like waving a bit of fresh liver before an uncaged mord and daring it to snap. Kincar sheathed his Star weapon and crossed the open space in one flying leap, his hands settling as he had aimed on the thief's shoulders. But what happened an instant after that was not part of his plan at all.

The stranger might have the size of a lad not yet half grown, but in that slight body was a strength that rivaled Kincar's. Startled as he must have been, he reacted automatically as one trained in unarmed combat. His shoulders shrugged, he wriggled, and, to Kincar's overwhelming astonishment and dazed unbelief, he found himself on the ground while the other stood over him, a knife blade stained with suard blood held at striking distance from his throat.

"Lie still, lowland rat"—the words were oddly accented but Kincar could understand them—"or you will speedily have two mouths—the second of my making!"

"Big talk, stealer of another man's meat!" Kincar glared back with what dignity he could muster from his position on the ground. "Have you never learned that only a hunter skins his own kill?"

"Your kill?" The manikin laughed. "Show me the wound with which you dealt that death, my brave-talking hunter, and I shall deliver you the meat."

"There are other ways of killing than by sword or spear."

The manikin's lips flattened against his teeth, drawing a little apart in a snarl.

"Aye, lowlander." He spoke more softly still, almost

71

caressingly. "There are such ways of killing. But your sort have them not—only the 'gods' kill so." But he spat after mouthing the word "gods" as a man might spit upon the name of a blood enemy. "And no 'god' would give a slave his power stick! You are naught but an outlaw who should be turned in for the price set upon him—to be used for the amusement of the 'gods' after their accursed way."

There had been outlaws in the Gorth of Kincar's birth. He could readily accept the idea that such men lived here also. But these "gods" were something else altogether. However, his immediate problem was to get safely out of the range of that knife, and his swift overthrow had given him a healthy respect for the one who now held it.

"I am no outlaw. I am a hunter. My mord flushed the suard in their feeding ground. One she slew, the other I killed as it fled. If you would have proof of that, look behind those bushes yonder where you will find the other made ready for packing. Or, better yet—" He whistled and the blade descended until he felt the chill touch of the metal on his throat.

"You were warned—" The manikin was beginning when Vorken swooped upon him. Only the overhang of his hood saved his face. As it was, the mord hooked claws in his jerkin and beat him about the head with her wings. Kincar rolled away and got to his feet before he called the mord off her victim. And ready in his hand now was the death rod of the Star Lords.

Vorken flapped up to a tree limb, her red eyes holding upon the manikin. But he lay on the ground, his attention all for the weapon Kincar had aimed at him. And his expression was the bleak one of a man facing inevitable death.

"Who are you, wearing the body of a slave, carrying

the death of a 'god'?" he demanded. "Why do you trouble the hills?"

Now that Kincar had his captive, he did not quite know what to do with him. To take a prisoner down to the hold, there to spy out their few numbers, their many lacks, would be folly indeed. On the other hand, to turn the man loose on the mountain, perhaps to arouse his own people, that was worse than folly. But to kill as a matter of expediency alone, that was an act Kincar could not commit.

Vorken stirred, uttering her warning, and a moment later they heard a musical whistle, unlike the shrilling of the mord. Kincar answered eagerly with the rest of the bar. The figure who tramped through drifted snow to join them did not come with Kincar's light hunter's tread. And at the sight of the silver clothing the manikin froze as a suard youngling might freeze under the shadow of a mord's wings—seeing raw death above it with no possible escape.

Lord Bardon, leading one of the pack larngs, came to a halt, the animal's head bobbing over his shoulder, the luck of the rest of the hunting party to be read in the small bundle lashed to its back. He surveyed the scene with open surprise.

"What have we here, Kincar?"

"A thief of another hunter's kill!" snapped the other. "Also a teller of tales. What else he may be, I have no knowledge."

The manikin's face was twisted with hate, whitened with something deeper than fear, a dull despair. But he made no answer, though his glance swung from the Star Lord to Kincar as if the last sight he expected to wonder over was such a friendly relationship between the two.

"Who are you?" Lord Bardon came directly to the

point, and then added—as if to himself—"and what are you, my small friend?"

But the manikin remained stubbornly silent. There was about him now the air of one about to be put to some torture, determined to endure to the end that he might not betray a weighty secret.

"He has a tongue." Kincar's exasperation broke out. "He was free enough with it before your coming, Lord—with all his talk of 'gods' and 'slaves'! But what he is or where he springs from I do not know. Vorken brought down a suard—a second, fleeing, I killed with the silent death. While I butchered Vorken's kill, he was busy here. And so I discovered him thieving—"

For the first time since Lord Bardon had appeared on the scene the manikin spoke.

"Aye, and but for that mord of yours, you'd have been meat, too, lowland dirt!"

"Perhaps so." Kincar gave credit where it was due. "He is a warrior, Lord, overturning me with some trick of fighting when I closed with him. But Vorken came, and I was free to use this—a threat he appeared to understand"—he held out the death tube—"though how that can be is a mystery—"

Lord Bardon's eyes were like light metal, cold, with a deadly luster in his dark face. "So he recognized a ray blaster. Now that is most interesting. I think it is important that he comes with us for a quiet talk together—"

The manikin had drawn his feet under him. Now he exploded for the nearest cover with the speed of a spear throw. Only this time Kincar was prepared. He crashed against the captive, bringing them both to the frozen ground with the force of that tackle. And when he levered himself up, the other lay so quiet that Kincar was for an instant or so very much afraid.

But the prisoner was only stunned, the rough handling leaving him tractable enough to be stowed away on the larng along with the meat. So encumbered they started back to the hold, making only one short side trip to look at the steam stream Kincar had chanced upon. Lord Bardon examined the carved chip and then looked to the trussed captive on the larng.

"Perhaps our friend here can tell us more concerning this. He is well clad, at home in these ranges, yet we have seen no other steading or hold. If they dwell within instead of without the mountains, that would explain it. But he is a breed new to me. How say you, Kincar; is he a dwarf of Gorthian breed?"

"I do not know, Lord. He seems not to be in any way misshapen, but rather as if it is natural with his kind to be of that size—just as I do not equal you in inches. There is in my mind one thing—the old song of Garthal s'Dar—" He began the chant of a native song-smith:

> "In the morning light went Garthal
> Sword in hand, his cloak about his arm.
> A white shield for his arm,
> And he raised his blade against the inner men,
> Forcing their chieftain into battle,
> Forcing them to give him freedom of their ways,
> That he might come upon his blood enemy
> And cross metal with him
> Who had raised the scornful laughter
> In the Hold of Grum at the Midyear feasting—

"The inner men," he repeated. "They were long and long ago—if they ever lived at all—for many of the old songs, Lord, are born from the minds of men and song-smiths and not out of deeds which really happened. But these 'inner men' were of the mountains, and they were small of body but large of deed, a warrior race of power. Or so Garthal found them—"

"And there are other tales of 'inner men'?"

Kincar grinned. "Such tales as one tells a youngling who would have his own way against the wisdom of his elders, warnings that should he not mend his ways the 'little men' will come in the dark hours and spirit him away to their hidden holds beneath the earth—from which no man ventures forth again."

"Aye," mused the Star Lord, "but in such tales there lingers a spark of truth at times. Perhaps the 'inner men,' who have vanished from the Gorth we knew, are not gone from here, and we have laid hands upon one. At any rate he will supply us with much which we should know for our own safety."

"I do not think this one will talk merely because we bid him."

"He shall tell us all he knows, which is of interest to us."

Kincar measured the greater bulk of the Star Lord. In his brown hands the manikin would be a girl child's puppet to be sure. Yet the half-blood shrank from the grim picture his imagination produced. To slay a man cleanly in battle was one thing. To mishandle a helpless captive was something far different—a thing he did not want to consider. But again it was as if the Star Lord had the trick of reading minds, for the other looked down at him with a hint of smile in his eyes, though there was no softening of the straight line of lip and jaw.

"We do not tear secrets from men with fire and knife, youngling—or follow outlaw tricks for the loosening of tongues!"

Kincar flushed. "Forgive, Lord, the ways of your people are as yet strange to me. I was reared in a hold of the mountains, not in Terranna. What do I know of Star Lord life?"

"True enough. But not 'your people,' Kincar, but 'my

people.' We are one in this as in all else, boy. You have an inheritance from us as well as from Styr—always remember that. Now let us bring this song-smith's hero into Dillan and the Lady Asgar and see what they can make of him to our future profit."

7

False Gods

Star Lord ways for extracting information from unwilling captives were indeed strange to Kincar, for questions were not asked at all. Instead their prisoner was given a seat before one of the heat boxes in the great hall of the old hold and left to meditate, though there were always those who watched him without appearing to do so.

After the first few minutes of lowering suspicion, the captive watched them openly in return, and his complete mystification was plain to read on his face. Something in their ways or bearing was too odd for him to comprehend. He stared wide-eyed at Lord Jon who was patiently teaching his half-Gorthian son the finer points of sword play before a fond and proud audience of the boy's mother and sister. They were both busy with their needles at the mending of undertunics—while the younger brother watched with the envious attention of one ready and willing to change places with the other boy at any moment.

And when the Lady Asgar came up behind Kincar and put a hand on his shoulder to gain his notice, the prisoner, seeing that friendly gesture, shrank in upon himself as if fearing some terrible outburst in return.

"This is a new thing you have found for us, younger

brother," she said. "Dillan is coming, though he is loathe to leave his calculations. So this is one you think might be straight out of the saga of Garthal the Two-sworded?"

"It is in my mind, Lady, that he is close to the song-smiths' recording of the 'inner men.' "

Vorken fluttered down from her chosen perch high in the roof to claw beseechingly at the Lady's cloak. Asgar laughed at the mord. "Now then, Vorken, would you have me in tatters because of your impatience? Being of the female kind yourself, you should know better than to tear clothing that can not easily be re-placed. Ha—up with you then, if that is how it must be." She stooped, and the mord sprang to her arm, climbing to her shoulder where she rubbed her head caressingly against the Lady's and chirruped in her ear.

"You have done very well this day, Vorken," Asgar continued as if the mord could understand every word she said. "More than your part. Now be patient, winged one, we have other business to hand."

But when she came to stand directly before the pris-oner, the manikin crouched low, drawing in upon him-self as if he would turn his body into a ball under the blows of a punishing lash. Nor would he lift his head to see eye to eye with the lady. His whole position suggested one awaiting death—and no easy passing at that. And it was in such contrast to the spirit with which he had faced Kincar that the latter was puzzled.

"So—what have we here?" Lord Dillan came to them, giving Kincar an approving pat upon the back as he passed. "This is your meat thief, boy?"

"He is more," remarked the Lady. "But there is a second mystery here. Why are we so fearsome to him?"

"Aye." Lord Dillan reached down and, with a hand gentle enough but with a force that could not be denied,

80

brought up the manikin's head so that he could see his face. The captive's eyes were squeezed shut. "Look upon us, stranger. We are not your enemies—unless you wish it so—"

That must have pricked like a sword point upon a raw wound. The eyes snapped open, but none of them were prepared for the black hate mirrored in their depths.

"Aye," the manikin snarled, "the 'gods' are never enemies—they wish the good of us all. Hear me, 'gods,' I give you homage!" He slipped from the pad to the floor, kneeling before the Star Lord. "You may slay me after your own evil fashion, 'gods,' but Ospik will not beg for his life!"

It was the Lady who spoke first. "There are no gods here, Ospik, nor do we have a liking for such titles even in jest. Why do you name us so?"

His broad mouth shaped a sneer he could not prevent, and his inner hatred fought against remnants of self-preservation. "How else should I name you—save as you have taught Gorth? You are the 'gods' from the far stars. Though what you do here in this ruin is beyond the imagining of a simple hunter. What you do here and with them—!" He pointed to Kincar, to the family of Lord Jon busy with their own concerns just out of earshot.

"Why should not kinsmen be together?" questioned the Lady softly.

"Kinsmen!" Ospik repeated the word incredulously. "But the young warrior is a lowlander, a Gorthian, and you are one of the 'gods'! There is no kinship between slave and master. To even think of such a blood-tie is red death for the slave!"

Lord Dillan's eyes had grown bleak and cold as he listened, and the hand that had continued to rest on Kincar's shoulder in the greeting of a comrade tightened its hold, crushing the scales of the younger man's shirt down on the flesh beneath as he stood steady under it. Only the Lady Asgar continued her inquiry with untroubled serenity.

"You are very wrong, Ospik. All those within this hold share a common heritage, at least in part. Those who seem to you Gorthian have also Star blood. Jon, whom you have been watching, is now schooling his eldest son, and that is his wife, his daughter, and his younger son—a large family for us. This is Kincar s'Rud." She indicated Kincar. "And Rud, his father, was brother to Dillan who stands before you. No slaves, no masters—kinsmen."

"Lord Rud's son!" Ospik's teeth showed in an animal snarl, and he gazed at Kincar as if he would spring full at the young man's throat in a mord's murderous attack. "Lord Rud with a slave son! Ho, that is fine hearing! So he has defiled himself has he—the great Rud himself has broken the first law of his kind? Good hearing—good hearing! Though no one shall ever hear it from my telling—" His head moved from side to side like the head of a cornered animal.

Kincar was bewildered, but he clung to the parts he understood. So Lord Dillan was close kin—somehow that was a thought to give warmth, a warmth as steady as if it arose from a heat box. But the manikin's talk of a Lord Rud who had broken the first law? How did Ospik know his father? Asgar spoke first.

"Rud, brother of Dillan, is dead, Ospik. He was killed almost twenty warm seasons ago when he went into a bitter water storm to save seamen trapped on a reef by the floundering of their ship—"

Ospik stared at her, and then he spat. "I am no addle-wit—not yet." Again his shoulders hunched under that unseen whip. "Lord Rud rules at U-Sippar, as he has since the memory of man. No 'god' would raise his shortest finger for the saving of a Gorthian out of the bitter water!"

The Lady Asgar caught her breath. "What have we found?" she demanded, clasping her hands together until the knuckles were hard knobs. "Into what kind of a Gorth have we come, Dillan?"

"To the one of our worst fears, it would seem," he made answer grimly. "The one which we perceived only palely and have always dreaded."

She gasped. "No, chance would not be so cruel!"

"Chance? Do you think that there is chance in this, Asgar? I would say it is part of a large design beyond our knowledge. We have striven to undo one wrong our kind wrought on Gorth. Here is another and far greater one. Shall we always be faced by the results of our troubling?"

Ospik had been looking from one to the other, glancing back at Lord Jon, at the others busy about their chosen tasks in the hall. Now he got to his feet, his hand outstretched to the two before him, his fingers curled about one another in a curious pattern.

"You are no 'gods'!" he accused shrilly. "You are demons who have taken on their seeming. By Lor, Loi, Lys, I bid you be as you really are."

Kincar answered that invocation with one of his own. "By Lor, Loi, and Lys, I tell you, Ospik, that these are Star Lords, though perhaps not of the kind you know. Could a demon remain while I say this?" And he repeated the sacred Three Lines in the older tongue he had been taught, feeling as he said them an answering warmth from the talisman he wore.

Ospik was shaken. "I do not understand," he said weakly. And Kincar would have echoed that, but he had sense enough to turn to Lord Dillan for an explanation.

"Ospik, we are truly of the Star blood." The Star

Lord's words had the impact of truth. "But we are not those whom you know. We have come from another Gorth. And in spirit we are opposed to the Lords of this world—or at least I would think it so from what you have told us."

"The 'gods' have done much here," Ospik returned, "but never for the good of Gorth. I do not know what mazed story you would tell me now—"

Later Kincar sat in the ring of warriors, half-blood and Star Lord gathered together, listening to Lord Dillan.

"That is the way of it! In this Gorth our kind brought a worse fate than the one we were fleeing from. Here our breed landed in arrogance and seized the country, making the natives slaves. All our wisdom was used to hold Gorth with a mailed fist. Only a few bands who have escaped to the wastes—or are native to those sections as are Ospik's people—are free. This is the evil Gorth that ours might have been."

"We are a handful against many." Lord Jon spoke musingly. "Yet this is in a manner our ill—"

"Aye, a handful. And this I say—which is only good war wisdom—we must make no moves until we know more of what lies here." That was Lord Bardon. He alone among the Star Lords in the hold had been born in the Star ships before the landing on Gorth. He had chosen to remain with this party because he had Gorthian children and grandchildren—a daughter sat in the circle of women to the left, two boys of her bearing were among the children.

Kincar was only half listening, being more set upon estimating the fighting strength of their party. Fifty in all had essayed the adventure of the gates. Twenty of these were women and young maids, ten were children. Of the remaining males eight were Star Lords, ranging from Lord Bardon to the young Lord Jon—

Sim, Dillan, Rodric, Tomm, Joc, and Frans. It was difficult to know their ages, but none of them had the appearance of a Gorthian past his fortieth summer. The mysterious change that had come upon their kind during the voyage across the void had set its seal heavy upon them.

The twelve swordsmen of half-blood were all young, but all tested fighting men, and Lord Jon's eldest son could soon be numbered among them. A good tough force—with such behind him no man would hesitate to foray. And the Star Lords had their own methods of fighting. Aye, had he been faced with an attack on a hold, Kincar would not have hesitated to raise his banner for a spear-festing.

But they were not going up against any hold or Gorthian force, they were to front Star Lords, twisted, vengeful Star Lords who used all of their secret learning to hold the rule of this world. And that was a very different thing. None of them here were so unblooded in war as to vote for a spear-festing before the full strength of the enemy could be ascertained.

However, they had won Ospik's support. The mountaineer, at first without comprehension, was at last forced to accept the evidence given him. Now he was eager for an alliance between his people and the hold party. It had been hard for him to think of Star Lords as friends, but once he could believe that comradeship possible, his agreement was wholehearted. And it was decided that he must return to his own hidden stronghold and promote a meeting between his Cavern Master and the others.

Before nightfall Ospik was on his way. But Kincar had a private puzzle of his own keeping him silent. He was in Cim's stall, spreading dried grass he had brought to bed down the larng, when a brighter gleam of light by the door told him he was no longer alone.

Lord Dillan noted with a nod of approval his efforts to make his mount comfortable.

"That is a good larng." There was a hesitancy in that opening. The Star Lord had come to speak on a subject far removed from the care of mounts, and Kincar sensed it.

"He is Cim." Kincar ran his hands caressingly about the pointed ears of the kneeling beast, stroking the callous spots where the reins rested. "I found him in the trapping pens, and he has been mine only since then."

Inside he was as shyly hesitant as Lord Dillan. Since that hour in Wurd's death chamber, when the tightly ordered existence that had always been his world had broken apart, when all security had been reft from him, he had tried to push aside the truth. It had been easier to accept exile from Styr, the prospect of outlawry, than to believe that he was not wholly Gorthian.

Now he did not want to face the fact that his father had been a man such as Dillan—perhaps resembling Dillan closely, since they had been brothers. Why—because he was afraid of the Star Lords? Or was it that he resented the mixture of blood that had taken from him the sure, ordered life of Styr? He never felt at ease in their company as did Jonathal, Vulth, and the others who had associated with the aliens from birth.

Perhaps his reluctance to acknowledge his mixed bloods was fostered by the fact that of all of them here in the hold, he alone had no outward marks of non-Gorthian heritage. Some of the others were taller than natives, others had eyes of a strange color, hair, features— And at a moment such as this, when he was forced to realize his bond with off-world kin, his first and strongest reaction was a wariness, the wariness of a man compelled to imposture and foreseeing exposure.

Dillan set the lamp he carried on the floor and leaned

86

back against the stall partition, his fingers hooked in his belt.

"Rud's son," he said quietly, giving the proper name the same unfamiliar turn of pronunciation he had given it at their first meeting.

"You do not see him in me!" blurted out Kincar.

"Not outwardly." When Dillan agreed so readily, Kincar had a pinch of nameless discontent. "But in other ways—"

Kincar voiced the question that had been in his mind all afternoon.

"Ospik says that a Lord Rud rules this district for the Star Lords. Yet how can that be? For if the Lord Rud who was my father is dead these many years— Another Lord—maybe a son of full Star blood?"

Dillan shook his head. "I think not. This is a tangle we had not thought to find. Perhaps in this Gorth there are counterparts of us—the selves we would have been had chance, or fate, or the grand design taken another road. But that would be a monstrous thing, and we would indeed be caught up in a nightmare!"

"How could a man face himself in battle?" Kincar had followed that thought to its logical end.

"That is what we must discover, youngling. Let it suffice that the Rud who rules here is not he who fathered you—nor could he be—"

"Aye, Ospik made it plain that in this Gorth Star Lord and native do not mate—"

"It is not that only." Dillan brushed the comment aside impatiently. "Nay, it is that the Rud who, by his way of life, his temperament, is content with things as they are in this world is not the Rud of our world. They would have no common meeting point at all. Rud was born in our Gorth three years after the landing of our ships, thus being my elder by a full twenty of warm seasons, the son of another mother. He had four ladies to wife—two of Star blood, two of Gorthian inheritance. Anora of Styr was his last, and she outlived him by less than a full year. He left behind him two sons and a daughter of full blood—they departed on one of the ships—and one of half-blood, you. But of you we were ignorant until Wurd sent us a message three months ago when he foresaw what might be your fate under Jord's enmity. He had kept you apart from us, wishing to make you wholly Gorthian that you might serve Styr the better, so that you have none of the common memories that might help you to adjust now. But Rud, your father, was rightly one to stand sword-proud, and glad we are that his blood lives on among us!"

"But you are of Rud's blood."

"Aye. But I am not as Rud. He was a warrior born, a man of action. And in a world of action that means much." Dillan smiled a little wearily. "I am a man of my hands, one who would build things I see in dreams. The sword I can use, but also do I most readily lay it aside. Rud was a mord on the hunt, ever questing for adventure. He was a sword-smith rather than a song-smith. But it is hard to describe Rud to one who knew him not, even when that one is his son." He sighed and picked up the lamp once more. "Let it rest that the Rud we knew was worth our allegiance—aye, our love. And keep that ever in your mind should fate force us to foray against this other Rud who holds false wardship in this Gorth—"

He lingered at the door of the stall. "You have made Cim comfortable. Come back to the hall now—we hold warrior-council in which each swordsman has a voice."

They ate in company, sharing the fruits of hunting and portions of their dwindling supplies with scrupulous accuracy. A hungry mord, Kincar recalled, was always the best hunter. No one here went so filled that he could not move mord-swift in attack. He chewed a mouthful of suard meat deliberately, savoring its fat-richness to the fullest extent.

The war council had come to a decision. They would hunt for the present, work to stock the hold with what supplies they could garner, perhaps trade with the inner men for extra foodstuffs. For the moment they would not venture forth from the valley guarded by the hold. They were far, Ospik had assured them, from the lowlands where the Star Lords of this Gorth kept control, where the might of strange weapons held slaves in hard bondage. But the thought of those who were their counterparts using such perverted power had driven the Lords into a brooding silence. And Kincar suspected that even were Lord Dillan to produce another gate, a new road to still another Gorth, he might not discover any among his peers willing to use it yet. They felt a responsibility for this world, a guilt for what the false lords did here.

Now they mounted a sentry in each of the watch-towers on the hold, marked out patrol paths for the morrow, divided duties between hunting and scouting among all the company, so that a man would alternate in each type of service.

When the meal was done, the Lady Asgar came to Kincar, in her hands one of the small singing-string boards of a traveling song-smith.

"Kincar, it is said that you have in song memory the saga of Garthal and his meeting with the 'inner men.' Since we have this day proven a part of that story to be no tale but the truth, do you now let us hear all of Garthal's spear-festing and the Foray of Loc-Hold."

He took the frame of the singing-strings on his knee shyly. Though he had played song-smith in Styr Hold, he had never thought to do so in such company as this. But "Garthal's Foray" was a song not too well known nowadays, though it had been a favorite of Wurd's and

Kincar had had good lessoning in its long swinging stanzas. Now he struck the two notes and began the rising chant—the tale of how Garthal went forth as a holdless man and came to Loc-Hold, and how he was later cheated of his fight-due so that he fled to the mountains with anger in his heart. Those about him, Lorpor, Vulth, Lord Jon, Jonathal, drew their swords and kept time with the sweet ting of blade against blade, while eyes shone in the lamplight and there were the voices of women bringing in the hum of undersong. Not since he had ridden out of Styr had Kincar known that sense of belonging.

8

First Foray

They had their meeting with the chief of the "inner men." He came warily and armed, with a covering guard who prudently prepared an ambush. All of these precautions proved to the men from the hold the deep-seated distrust of, and hatred held for, the alien rulers of the plains by the native Gorthians. But at the conclusion of their council, the chief had been forced to admit that there were now two kinds of Star Lords in his land, and the later-come variety were not the wrathful "gods" he had always known. He did not go so far as to reveal any of the details of his own keep, though he did agree to a measure of trade—to supply dried fruits and coarse meal for one of the inexhaustible star torches.

The "inner men" were by long training fine workers in metal. They produced, for the admiration of the hold, coats of ring mail, fine, deceivingly light in weight—but, unfortunately, fashioned only to fit the small bodies of their own race, as were their beautifully balanced swords, which were too light and too short of hand grip for the newcomers. Lord Bardon, surveying these regretfully, went on to other plans. And the next day when he was in the hunting field with Kincar, he suggested that Vorken be set about the business of marking down game, while the younger man aid him in a different search.

"A sapling?" puzzled Kincar. "For a new kind of spear shaft, maybe? But such as we seek now would be too slender, would break at the first thrust which had any power behind it."

"Not a spear. It is intended for another weapon, one from the older days on the Star world from which our fathers came. It was a favorite there of primitive men, but it was so well used that the old tales say it gave him an advantage over warriors clad in mail."

At the end of the day they returned to the hold with a good selection of different varieties of tough yet resilient wood lengths lashed upon the larng-burden of meat for the pot. Vorken, not being under obligation to consider the worth of saplings, had proved a more alert hunter than the men.

Since Lord Bardon had only hazy memory to guide him in the manufacture of the new weapon, they spoiled many lengths of wood, choosing others badly. However, at the end of three days they produced crude bows. Arrows followed. They learned, mainly by mistakes, the art of proper heading and feathering. Now three quarters of the population of the hold had taken a hand in the work, and the hall after the fall of night was a fletcher's workroom.

They discovered that the pull of the bows depended upon the strength of an individual—that the mighty six-foot shaft that served Lord Bardon could not even be strung by any half-blood, while Kincar—with a smaller and lighter weapon—could hit the mark in the trials just as accurately and speedily, though perhaps with not the great penetrating force of the Star Lord.

Oddly enough, only Lord Bardon, Lord Jon, and Lord Frans among the full-bloods showed any proficiency with the bow, and there was much good-humored banter aimed at their fellows who were unable to turn marksmen by will alone.

"Too long at machines," Lord Bardon observed as Dillan's arrow went woefully wide of the mark for the third time in succession. "This is no matter of pushing a button; it needs true skill."

Lord Dillan laughed and tossed the bow to its owner. "A skill not in *my* hand or eye it is certain. But we cannot say that of our brothers."

For, as the full-bloods found it something to be laboriously learned, the half-bloods took to archery with a readiness that suggested that the Three must have given them the gift at birth, to lay dormant waiting this moment. From practice at a stationary mark set up in the courtyard, they advanced to hunting, and the rewards came in an upshoot of meat supplies and the growing pile of suard skins to be plaited into cloaks and robes against the chill of the storm winds.

The cold weather had closed in upon them with true harshness. There was one period when they were pent for five days within the hold, the snow-filled blasts sealing the outer world from them. Any plans for scouting into the lowlands must wait upon more clement days.

Lord Dillan and his assistants had to set aside their work on the machine intended to open a gate upon another Gorth. Too many essential elements had been destroyed with the other gates. And, in spite of their questioning of the inner men's smiths and metal miners, some of those could not be rediscovered even in the crude state of unworked ore. They did not speak of this within the hold, though it was generally known. Instead, men began to plan ahead for a lengthy stay there. Talk arose of working the fields in the deserted valley. Surely land that once had supported a large community would provide a living for their own limited numbers.

At last came a lull between storms, when the sun was dazzlingly reflected from the crusted snow and the trees cast wide blue shadows across the ground. It was a day when the crisp air bit at the lungs as a man inhaled, but at the same time set him longing to be out in the open.

Kincar stood on the crown of one watchtower, with Vorken marching back and forth along the waist-high parapet before him, stretching wide her wings and giving harsh voice to her own private challenge. This was the season when the mords of the hatcheries took mates, and Vorken was lonely as she had never been. It would seem that in this Gorth her kind were either uncommon or had never evolved from the large and vicious menaces of the mountain heights.

She was so restless that Kincar was worried. Should she go out in search of her kind, she might well never return. Yet he knew that if he tried to restrain her by caging, her restlessness would develop into a wild mania centered only upon escape, and she might beat herself to death against the walls of her prison. In order to keep her, he must leave her free, holding to the hope that she would come back at some time of her own choosing.

With another eerie cry, she gave a leap that carried her up and out, climbing in a tight spiral until he could not see her at all. He beat his cold-numbed hands against his thighs, striding back and forth to keep his feet free from the frost-deadening chill as he waited. But there was no Vorken planing down wind, no shrilling whistle. It was as if the mord had gone out through some hole in the sky.

"She is gone?" Snow crunched under Lord Bardon's

boots. "I thought the wild fever must be on her when I saw her this morning."

"I couldn't cage her," Kincar argued in his own defense. "Without a hatchery she would have gone mad in a cage."

"True enough. And, though we have not sighted any of her breed here, boy, that is no reason to think that they do not exist. Perhaps in the lowlands she will discover a hold with a hatchery."

That was poor comfort, but it was the only hope he had to hold to. And he knew that in setting her free he had saved her life.

"To lay bonds upon any unwilling living thing, whether it be man or beast, is evil." Lord Bardon rested his hands upon the parapet and stood looking down the cleft of the entrance valley toward the plains. If all they had heard was true, there lay a bondage far worse than the alliance between trained mord and hunter. "Service must be rooted in the need to form part of a pattern. In that way it is security of mind—if not always of body. Vorken serves you in some ways, and you in exchange give her the returns she wants. At present she must be left free for what is important to her, as is right. And now, Kincar," he glanced down with a smile, "I have a service to offer you. After many delays our friends of the inner mountain have decided that they may offer us a measure of trust. They have sent a message that they will show us a sheltered and secret way to look upon one of the main highways of the lower country and assess the traffic that passes there."

"In this weather?"

"It would seem that the cold season does not hit so heavily in the plains as it does here. Also the Lords of the lowlands have their reasons for keeping the lines of communication open. Where men live in distrust and fear, speedy travel is oftentimes a necessity. But, at any rate, we shall be able to see more than we do from here. And if you wish, you may ride with us."

The party from the hold was a small one. Ospik and one of his fellows, Tosi, served as guides. Behind them rode Lord Bardon, his huge bow slung over his shoulder to point a warning finger into the sky, Lord Frans, Jonathal, and Kincar. They were mounted on larngs who protested with muttering grumbles against being urged into the cold, and they led one of the burden breed to carry provisions and additional robes, lest they be storm-stayed out of shelter.

Ospik's trail led to the side of the mountain near which Kincar had charted the warm rill, and then it zig-zagged crookedly back and forth in a dried water-course where many rock piles made the footing so chancy they dismounted and led their beasts. The path, if so it could be termed, ended in a screen of brush before the mountain wall. But that screen was not what it appeared, for they pushed through it into a dark opening that might have been a deep running crevice.

But, as they advanced and Lord Bardon triggered a torch to light them, Kincar marked the signs of the tools that had turned a fault of nature into a passage for men. However much it had been wrought to provide a way through the mountain caverns, it was not one much used by the community of indwellers. As they threaded their way along it into a cave that fanned far out into deep darkness, their light bringing to life sparkles of answering fire from crystals on the walls, and then to another narrow passage and more caverns opening into one another, they met no one else, heard no sounds save the murmur of water—and those arising hollowly from their own footfalls. The whole mountain range, Kincar marveled, must be honeycombed with cave, crevice, and cavern, and the indwellers had made use of them to their own advantage.

Once they edged perilously over a narrow span set in place to cross a steaming hot flood, their heavier bodies and the bulk of the larngs going one at a time over a bridge made for manikins, choking and coughing as they passed from the fumes of the boiling water. And once or twice they caught a whiff of carrion reek, a distant rustle, as if some nightmare creature had crawled aside from their way, unable to dispute the light of the torch.

Time had no meaning here. They might have spent only hours, or a full day in the depths. Twice they halted to rest and eat, both times in grottoes of prismatic crystal, cupped in a circle of fire-hearted jewels, with the lace-tracery, formed by countless centuries of drip, making palace screens and drapery. It was a world Kincar had never conceived of being, and he explored with Jonathal, each pointing out to the other some particular wonder before or above. Fountains frozen before their spray streamed away, a tree, a fruit-heavy vine, they were all to be found. And in company with those were creatures out of a song-smith's dreams— fair, grotesque, horrible.

Ospik laughed at their surprise, but kindly. "These are to be found many places elsewhere." A pride of possession colored his words. "And many far better. There is our Hall of Meeting—"

"Jewels in the wall!" Jonathal touched a flashing point on a copy of a tree limb.

Their guide shook his head. "Jewels, aye, are to be found. But none of these are real gems, only bits of rock crystal. Take them away from the cavern and you will have nothing remarkable."

"But—" Kincar burst out—"to think of this buried under the earth!"

Lord Frans smiled. He had not moved about, but sat cross-legged, his back against the haunches of his resting larng. However, he had been studying what lay about them with some measure of the same eagerness.

"It is the earth which formed this, Kincar. And, as Ospik has said, tear this out of its present setting and the magic would be gone from it. It is indeed a wonder worth traveling far to see." He drew a small tablet from his belt pouch and with a stelo made a swift sketch of the frozen vine.

When they went on from that last cavern of crystal, the way was again dark, the walls crannied. Kincar forgot his amazement in a growing tension. He glanced now and again over his shoulder. Though he never saw anything but the familiar outline of Cim and, behind the mount, a glimpse of Lord Frans, yet he was plagued with a sense of being watched, a feeling that if he could only turn quick enough he would see something else—and not a good thing.

His hand was at his breast, flattened above the Tie lying there. That touch was not to assure the safety of the talisman but to reassure himself—as if from the Tie he drew a feeling of security against that invisible lurking thing.

The passage now sloped upward, so that they climbed. Tool marks on the walls spoke of the labor that had gone into the opening of this way, but it was a narrow one, so that they went one after the other, and some outcrops of rock in the roof forced both Star Lords and larngs to stoop, the stone brushing the crests on the others' helms.

After one last steep ascent they came into a cave, wide, but with a small opening through which had entered a drifting point of snow and beyond which they could hear the whistling wind of the outer world.

Ospik trotted to this door and stood there, sniffing as might some burrow creature suspicious of the freedom beyond. "Wind up—but no storm," he reported with assurance. "By sunup you will have a fine perch from which to go a-spying. But that is some hours off, so take your ease."

Tosi had already gone to a section well out of line with the cave mouth. And he busied himself there pulling from a crevice a supply of dry and seasoned wood, some light and white as old bones, which he kindled by a coal carried in a small earthenware box, making a fire they crouched about. At last, wrapped in their fur cloaks, the larngs forming a wall of animal heat to reflect the fire, they dozed away what was left of the night.

The cavemouth faced northeast, so that the dawn light was partly theirs, making a warning of gray when Kincar was shaken gently awake by Jonathal. He rubbed smarting eyes and swallowed bites from the journeycake pushed into his hand. They left their mounts in the cave, Tosi volunteering as larng tender. Then the four from the hold, with Ospik still as guide, went out upon a broad ledge and found themselves on a mord's perch above a valley.

There was snow here, sculptured by the wind. But in one strip it had been beaten down, mushed with dark streaks of soil into a grimy path. And it must have required a goodly amount of travel to and fro to leave such well-defined traces. Yet the surrounding country was wild, with no other evidences of civilization.

"Your road to the plains," Ospik pointed out. "For those who use it, you must wait, Lords. Those who travel it do only by daylight."

So they drew lots for the post of lookout, and the rest went back to the shelter of the cave. Kincar, having the first watch, amused himself with the laying out of an ambush plan, such as Regen might have done. This was a proper place for such, armed as they were with the bows. For man-to-man combat after the old fashion it would not have served so well. Here on the ledge one could stand and pick off all lead men in a first surprise, leaving any force below without an officer to rally about.

The snow deadened sound, and a cortege came into view with a sudden appearance, which shamed Kincar out of his notion of himself as a seasoned warrior. His warning hiss brought out the others to creep across the ledge.

Kincar, used to traders' caravans with their lumbering goods wains, or the quick trot of mounted warriors, watched the present party amazed. There were men mounted on larngs to be sure, Gorthians—though there were differences in arms and clothing to be observed. Yet behind that first clot of riders came something else. Two burden larngs clumped along about ten feet apart, and linking the first to the second was a chain of metal. From this issued at spaced intervals—in pairs—other chains, smaller. And each of those—there were four pair of them—ended in collars, the collars clamped about the throats of stumbling, reeling, moaning figures.

A second pair of larngs so linked, towing more prisoners, came into view. One of the captives fell, was dragged along the ground. A rider trotted up, and a whip swung with the intention of maximum pain to the fallen. But, in spite of the blows rained upon him, the fallen one did not stir. There was a shout, and the larngs halted while the riders held a conference.

"Who are those?" Lord Frans demanded hotly of Ospik.

The mountain dweller regarded them slyly from the corners of his eyes.

"Outlaws or slaves—ones who fled from the plains and are now being returned to their homes. The lucky ones die before they reach there."

The rider who had used the whip now slid from his pad and unhooked the collar of the captive. He jerked the body aside, then kicked, and the limp form rolled into a ditch.

There was no need for spoken agreement, for any order, among the four on the ledge. Bow strings came back in unison, twanged as four hands reached for a second arrow, eyes already on a new mark.

A scream, a hoarse, startled cry, the clash of metal against metal as a sword was drawn. But four of the slave guards were down, and one of the chained captives had seized upon the whip, using its stout butt to twist at his prisoning bonds.

It was a slaughter rather than a battle. And the archers proved the worth of their weapons over and over again, shooting larngs so that the riders could not flee. Ospik leaned perilously close to the rim of the ledge watching the deaths below with glistening, hungry eyes.

Twice the guards turned on their captives to kill. And both times they died before their blows went home. In the end only those chained to the dead burden larngs were still alive. Ospik spoke first.

"Now that was a mighty killing, Lords—a mord feeding as shall be remembered long. But it will also bring boiling out those to hunt us down in turn."

Lord Bardon shrugged. "Is there a path down from this sky perch of yours, Ospik? We needs must see what can be done for those wretches below."

"If your head is clear, you can take it!" The mountaineer dropped over the lip of the ledge, hung for a moment by his hands, and then went from one hold to another as if he were a wall insect. The others followed him, much more slowly, and with—at least on Kincar's part—some misgivings.

9

Volunteer

They came out of the brush into the open space bordering the road.

"When the prisoners are loose," ordered Lord Bardon, "collect what arrows you can."

"Now that is indeed wisdom, Lord." Ospik gave tribute. "Let the wild beasts feast here, and no one can say clearly what was the manner of these men's death."

Jonathal had plunged ahead and was prowling about among the bodies of the guards, examining their belts. Now he called and held up a locking rod. But, as they all started toward the chained ones, the man who had worked vainly with whip butt to break his way free gave a wailing cry and crouched, his eyes wild with hate. The whip lash sang out, striking Lord Frans's arm. Lord Bardon jerked his companion out of lash range.

"We should have thought. Take cover, Frans! To these we are the devils they fear the most!"

Jonathal used the lock-rod on the chain, freeing it first from the dead larngs. The half-dazed captives went into action, pulling it back between them, slipping their collar chains out of its hold. They were still paired by the collars, but they were no longer fastened between the slain animals.

For the most part they hunched in the snow, blinking stupidly, their spurt of energy exhausted in that one act, save for the whip wielder who got to his feet and faced his Gorthian rescuers with a spark of spirit. His face was swollen, with angry cuts under smears of dried blood. He might have been of any age, but he handled himself as might a trained warrior, and his head was up. Broken and bruised he was in body, perhaps, but not in spirit.

"What do you?" the words came haltingly, mumbled, as puffed and torn lips moved over broken teeth.

Jonathal wrenched a cloak from one of the dead guards and threw it around a shivering woman before he answered.

"We make you free."

The man turned his battered face so that his one open eye went from Jonathal to Kincar. Apparently all intelligence and curiosity had not been ground out of him by ill treatment. But neither was he willing or able to accept them readily as friends. Kincar gave the best proof of peaceful intentions he could think of, pulling a sword from the scabbard of the nearest guard and holding it out, hilt foremost.

That one unswollen eye widened in disbelief, and then a hand shot out, clawed about the hilt, and spun it out of Kincar's lax hold. The man panted as if he raced up the mountain.

"That is the way of it," Jonathal approved. "Get free, get a blade in your hands. And it is up swords and out at them!"

But Kincar believed that the captive did not hear that at all. He was too busy using the hard knob on the sword hilt to pry at his chains. Most of the others were apathetic, and all bore such marks of ill usage, men and women alike, that Kincar fought a rising nausea as he worked at the stubborn collars. Then Jonathal chanced upon some trick of their locking, and after that they tossed them aside. A few of the released made for the bodies of the guards, raiding for provision bags. And Kincar and Jonathal, much as they disliked the task, had to struggle with the weak creatures to see a fair sharing out of the food.

Kincar was on his knees beside a woman, trying to coax her to taste the coarse meal bread she held in her hand and stared at with a pitiful blankness as if she could not connect it with food, when the man to whom he had given the sword came up. He now wore a guard's armor jerkin and a helmet, and he was sucking a strip of dried meat, unable to attack it with his teeth. But he carried the sword, unsheathed in his other hand. And he watched Kincar warily.

"Who are you?" he mumbled, but in that muffled voice there was the snap of command. "Why did you do this?" The bare blade gestured at the littered road, where the dead were being stripped for the advantage of the living.

"We are those who are enemies to any rule which sets men in chains." Kincar chose his words carefully. "If you would know more, come to our leader—"

"With the point of this resting between your shoulders will I come." The blade caught the light of the rising sun.

"Well enough." Kincar pulled a robe about the woman and stood up. "My hands are open, hold captain." He gave the man the title that seemed to match his manner.

Without looking to see if he did follow, Kincar walked to the screen of bushes where the Star Lords had taken cover. But another had sought that same way before him. As Kincar thrust aside leafless limbs, he saw Lord Bardon and Lord Frans with Ospik, who was passing across arrows he had collected. Only, the

105

three intent upon that reckoning were not alone there. One of the guards had survived the attack, not only survived it but had traced the source of that sudden death.

Perhaps the surprise of seeing who had led it—Star Lords—had kept him quiet at first. But now he crouched behind Lord Bardon, concentrated fury plain to read on his sleek face, a slender needle-knife ready in his hand. And Kincar, knowing very well how that murderous weapon was used by an expert, threw himself forward.

He struck the lurking guard waist high, but he did not carry him to the ground as he had planned. The fellow wriggled in his grasp, loose enough to strike down at Kincar with the knife intended for Lord Bardon's throat. Kincar's hand closed about that swooping wrist just in time, halting the blow when the point was almost into his flesh, kicking out to upset the other's balance. Fire scored down the side of his underchin; then the blade caught in the top of his scale coat and snapped. Before the jagged end of the blade could reach his eyes as the other struck, they were torn apart by a grip neither could hope to break. The hands that had pulled Kincar loose released their hold.

"He got you, boy!"

Blood dripped on Kincar's chest, trickling down over his surcoat. Then Lord Bardon's fingers under his chin forced his head up and to one side as the other assessed the damage.

"A scratch only, thanks be!" the Star Lord exploded a moment later. "We'll get a pack on that to stop bleeding and you'll live, youngling—" There was relief close to laughter in his voice. But when he spoke again, his voice was ice hard. "Put that one in storage, Frans. He can answer some useful questions. And"—engaged in pushing Kincar back against the face of the cliff so he could get at his wound, Lord Bardon sighted the ex-slave who had followed the younger man—"where did *you* spring from?"

"He was one of the prisoners." Kincar got out that much of an explanation before Lord Bardon's fingers, busy with a dressing, pressed him into silence.

"And he would like to see the color of our blood," suggested Lord Frans. He had trussed the guard efficiently, leaving him lying at the foot of the rise. Now he stood empty-handed facing the newcomer.

But if the man had come with swift death for his overlords in his mind, he did not move to attack now. To read any expression on his torn and battered face was impossible, but he stood watching Lord Bardon's hasty work with bandage pack, his eye flitting now and again to the cursing prisoner, his late guard. When he spoke, it was to ask the same question he had earlier made to Kincar.

"Who are you?" Then he made his bewilderment clear in a rush of words. "You wear the guise of the Black Ones, yet you have slain their loyal men, released us who are condemned slaves. Now you tend the wound of a lowlander as if he were a kinsman. And the guard, who is one of your followers, dealing death and torment at your command, lies in bonds. I ask again, who are you?"

"Let us say that we are those who have been sent to put an end to trouble in this land. Though we bear the outward seeming of your rulers, we are not of their kind. Can you believe that?"

"Lord, I have witnessed three great marvels this day. I have seen the despoiling of a slave train; I have seen men of my race and Dark Ones move with a common purpose as kinsmen, with a care for one another as true battle comrades have. And I have seen one set in rule over us laid in bonds by you. Can one who has seen

107

such deeds as these *not* believe? And now that I have looked upon you fairly, I can testify that you are not as the Dark Ones—though you wear their bodies. By Lor, Loi, and Lys—" he went to one knee and held out his sword, hilt extended to Lord Bardon—"I am your man—I who swore by the Forest Altars never to render service to any outland lord."

Lord Bardon touched the sword hilt, but he did not take it into his hand, and the other's eye shone. He was accepted by fealty and not as a bondsman, and Lord Bardon's knowledge of that ceremony impressed him still more deeply.

He was on his feet once more, the sword slammed smartly into sheath.

"I await orders, Lord—"

That reminded Lord Frans of the problem to hand. "We can't just turn these people loose on the country-side. They would die or be scooped up by another patrol."

"What about it, Ospik," Lord Bardon asked the mountaineer. "Will your chief suffer us to take such a party through the ways?"

Ospik plucked at his lower lip. "You have struck a smart blow at the 'gods,' outlander. But, suppose those are taken again, they will blat out all they know and speedily. All men talk when the 'gods' will it. We have kept our land because its secrets were not known—"

"Once they are in the valley of the hold, Ospik, I do not think they will fall prey again."

Ospik nodded. "There is that to consider. But I have not the final word; I can but be a messenger. Come you with me and speak to our chief yourself."

"And in the meantime? What if there is another body of guards along this way?" asked Lord Bardon.

"As to that—get these back into the shelter of a side

gulch here. It is a place you can easily defend if the need arises, and it is out of sight."

So they brought the released prisoners, the possessions of the guards, anything that might be of use to the captives, into a small side valley Ospik showed them. Archers on the heights above might well hold that camp against a strong attack. And they remained there as Bardon went back with Ospik into the mountain ways.

The shock of the captives' sudden change in fortune was beginning to wear away and a handful of the men bestirred themselves, under the command of the man Lord Bardon had enlisted, to shepherd the less alert of their fellows and arm themselves from the spoil of battle. Seeing that their leader appeared to have matters well in hand, the three from the hold remained aloof, save when physical help was needed. But when the temporary camp was in some sort of order, the leader came to them, saluting Lord Frans with upheld palm.

"We are at your command, Lord. Though perhaps you do well not to walk among us until those know you better for what you are. For their fear and hate for those you resemble—in outward form—runs high, and it is seldom that we have a chance to approach a Dark One within sword distance. Someone, with dulled wits and a good reason, might well attempt to try your deathlessness with metal—"

"But you do not think as do they?"

"Nay, Lord. I am Kapal, once Band-leader to free men of the wastes—until I was trapped and collartamed (or so they thought) by the Hands of the Dark Ones. We have fought, and hid, and fought again ever since the Dark Ones sent to enforce their rule upon the fringes of the Barren Lands. Mostly we die, our blades in hand, cut down in battle. We are very few now. When they took Quaar, they left but a handful of posts, and these can be overrun one by one, as they will do. We die, but we die free! Only"—his eye flickered from Lord Frans to the tall bow the Star man carried—"mayhap with weapons such as these to kill silently and at a good distance, men need not die so hopelessly any more."

"It may be so. We shall see—"

Kapal manifestly took that as a promise of a brighter future. "Let me out into the Barren Lands, Lord, with such a hope to voice, and I shall bring you a hundred hands of good men to ride beneath your banner! I can be gone within the hour if you wish."

"Not so. It is not given to me to have the ordering of this matter, Kapal. And what of these?" Lord Frans pointed to the late captives. "Are any among them minded to raise blade against their late masters?"

"Perhaps they are so minded," Kapal admitted. "But most of them are broken in spirit. Two, mayhap three of them could rally to a battle call. The rest—" He shrugged. "They have worn the collar chain too long."

"So do I think also. But what if they are given a measure of safety, a stretch of land where they may rest without fear, will they sow seed and reap, hunt meat, and work thus for a community that does not ask sword service in return?"

"That they might well do, Lord. If you know of such a place—safe from the Dark Ones' raids. But then you must have come from there!" He glanced from Lord Frans to Kincar and Jonathal. "It is plain to see that these, your guardsmen, have never known the bite of chain or whip, and yet they wear not a Hand's brand upon them—"

"A Hand's brand—?"

"Aye, lord. Those who are one in spirit with the Dark Ones bear their seal for all men's seeing. Look you!"

110

He crossed to the prisoner. The former guard spat filth, but Kapal stooped to fasten fingers in the other's hair, holding up his head and pointing to a mark just above and between the other's brows. Set deep in the skin was the brand left by hot metal, a small, threefold figure familiar to Kincar, to Jonathal—but reversed! And at that blasphemy both of the half-bloods raised fingers in the blessed sign to repudiate such vileness. Kapal saw their gesture, and when Lord Frans echoed it, he burst forth:

"The Three—you give service to the Forest Ones, Lord?"

"I give service to a belief of my own, of which the Three are another manifestation, Kapal. Good thoughts and beliefs have the respect of any man, whether they be his own by birth, or native to his friends and kinsman. But here, I think, a certain symbol has been deliberately used vilely—"

"That is true, Lord. For those who serve the Dark Ones with their full will allow themselves to be marked thus, and take pride in it—so that all others may see it and fear them. But there are those who do not fear, rather do they hate!" He loosened his hold, and the prisoner's head fell back to the ground.

"It follows a very old pattern." Lord Frans spoke more to himself than to those about him. "Sneer at and degrade what might be a banner of hope to the slave. Aye, an old, old pattern. It is a ripe time for the breaking of such patterns!"

They were never to know what argument Lord Bardon used successfully with the ruler of the inner mountain in behalf of the rescued slaves. But in the late afternoon he returned with the message that they might use the passages to take the company to the hold valley. It was a long, slow trip. And they had left two heaped piles of stones to mark graves in the gulch. The

111

woman Kincar had tried to coax into eating was gone, and with her an old man whose wits wandered so that none of his companions in misfortune knew his name or where he had been taken.

More than a day was spent on that journey, for they had to rest many times, the larngs carrying the weakest when the passages permitted riding. The men Kapal had indicated as being worth recruiting for spearfesting formed a unit under the wasteland leader, accepting his commands readily, and they alone of the rescued were interested in their strange surroundings.

The prisoner stayed in the hands of the hold party, his safety was only assured with them. But, as they penetrated deeper into the winding ways underground, his defiance seeped out of him and he was willing enough to stay very close to his captors, tagging either Kincar or Jonathal as if he were a battle comrade.

At the fifth rest period Lord Bardon called Kincar to him. "By Ospik's reckoning we are now not too far from the entrance in the hold valley. Tosi will go with you as a guide; take your larng and ride for aid. Many of these are close to collapse and we cannot carry them to the hold. Get extra mounts and more food—"

So it was that they brought the weary party into the fortress where the freed slaves, their wounds dressed, their hunger eased, sat for the most part in dumb bewilderment around the heating units, staring with dull surprise at the life about them. But the Lord Dillan called a council of war in the upper chamber he had taken for his own—and to this Kapal alone of the rescued was summoned.

"The guard is wide open to probe," Lord Dillan said of their prisoner. "Doubtless that is used regularly upon him by his masters. The man he was—he might have been—was destroyed when they set that brand upon him. By that act he surrendered his will and they can use him as they wish. It is a horrible thing!"

"So we agree. But we cannot concern ourselves too deeply now with what has been done in the past. We must think of what lies before us. The question is, dare we, with our few numbers, make any move against the entrenched strength of these tyrants?" asked Lord Bardon.

Lord Jon broke the long moment of silence. He was the youngest of the Star Lords, perhaps by their reckoning as youthful and as inexperienced as Kincar had been in the company of Wurd and Regen. Now he asked a simple question.

"Dare we *not?*"

Lord Dillan sighed. "There it is. Being what we are, striving toward the goal we have set for ourselves, we must interfere."

"Aye. But not foolishly, throwing away any advantage we may have," Lord Bardon cut in. "We must make our few count as well as an army. And we must know more of the lowlands before we venture there. Wring that guard dry of all he knows, Dillan. And let us set a post on that road, take what toll we can from other slave trains passing. Then—send a scout into the lowlands— Kapal!"

Soothing dressings about the outlaw's head covered all but one eye and his mouth, but he arose limberly.

"Kapal, what are the chances of a scout into the lowlands?"

"Few and ill, Lord. They have control posts along every road, and all travelers must account for themselves. To one who knows not the land it is impossible."

Lord Bardon corrected him. "Nothing is impossible. It is merely that the right way is not clear at first. Supposing a Dark One was to travel, would any dare question him?"

Kapal shook his head. "Lord, the Dark Ones *never* travel. Death comes not to them through age, but metal enters their flesh as easily as it does ours. They live well protected and only go forth from their hold in air-flying wains, the magic of which they alone know. Just one sort of man would dare such a scout—"

"And that?"

"One bearing the mark of evil—he could pretend to be a messenger."

Kincar's hand sought what he wore secretly. His eyes went from man to man about that circle, studying each in turn. Already he knew the answer. Of all the hold party he was the only one showing no trace of alien blood. The scout could only be his.

"I will go—"

He did not realize that he had said that aloud until he saw Lord Dillan look at him, caught the grim approval in Lord Bardon's appraisal. His hand was at his lips, but it was too late.

10

Storm, Night, and the Shrine

Kincar stood at one of the narrow windows in the Lady Asgar's chamber. The sky as seen through that slit showed clear rose. It was going to be a fair day, and the wind that swept the snow from the courtyard had died away.

"Is it not a matter of time?" he asked without turning his head.

There was no answer, for there was only one they could make, and so far they did not voice it.

"You cannot do it—not and still wear the Tie." Lord Dillan put into words what Kincar had known for long hours since he had made that impulsive offer. "I am not sure you could do it in any case. Such an act might cause an unthinkable traumatic shock—"

Now Kincar faced around. "It is a mark only."

"It is a mark which negates everything in which you believe. And for one bearing the Tie—"

But for the first time in long minutes the Lady Asgar moved. "This devil's mark must be set upon its victims with some ceremony. And the very ritual of that ceremony impresses its meaning upon the new servant of evil. It is a thing of the emotions, as all worship—whether of light or dark forces—is a matter of emotion.

115

If a thing is done without ceremony, or if it is done in another fashion altogether—"

"You mean?"

"That mark is made with a metal branding rod, is it not? Well, it is in my mind to reproduce its like another way—without ceremony. And while it is done Kincar must think upon its falseness and the reasons for his accepting it. Let him hold the Tie in his two hands and see if it repudiates him thereafter."

He crossed to her eagerly. "Lady, let us try!" If this was the answer, if he could have the mark without suffering inner conflict—

She smiled at him. "I have many forms of magic, Kincar. Let us see if my learning reaches so far. Do you hold the Tie now and think upon what you would do for us and why. If all goes well, we shall transform you into the seeming of an obedient Hand."

He was already clad in the alien trappings of one of the slave guards, assembled from their loot of the road attack. Now he brought out the smooth stone that was his legacy and trust from Styr's lord. With it between his palms, he whispered the words of Power, feeling the gentle glow which answered that invocation. And then he closed his eyes.

Concentrating upon the Tie he waited. His flesh tingled under a pressing touch upon his forehead. Three times that pressure. Then nothing at all. The Tie was quiescent, nor had it gone dead as he feared.

"Is that it?" asked the Lady Asgar.

"That is it!" Lord Dillan replied.

Kincar opened his eyes and laughed. "No change. The Tie did not change!"

Lord Dillan released pent breath in a sigh. "You had the right of it, Asgar. He is free to go. Give her the Talisman, Kincar, it will be well guarded—" But he paused at Kincar's shake of the head.

"Not so, Lord. It has not repudiated me. Therefore, it is still my trust and I cannot resign it elsewhere."

"If it is found on you, if they so much as suspect you wear it—! The result might be worse than you can imagine. In our Gorth it must be borne secretly, though there it was an object of reverence. What would it be here?"

But Kincar was restoring it to the usual place of concealment beneath his clothing. "All that may be true, Lord. I only know that I cannot render it up to anyone unless it is ready to go. That is the nature of a Tie. Were I to leave it here, I would be drawn back speedily, my mission unaccomplished. It is a part of me until my guardianship is done, which may come only at my death—or earlier if it is so willed."

"He is right." The voice of the Lady Asgar held a troubled note. "We have never learned the secret of the Ties, as you know. It is his trust and his fate. And somehow"—she hesitated and then added her last words with a rush—"it may be his salvation also!"

Together they went through the hall into the court-yard. It was a very early hour, and no one noted their passing. Cim was padded and ready. And Kapal walked the larng slowly back and forth.

"You have the map?" he asked as Kincar took the reins from him and swung up on the mount. "Think again, young lord, and let me take on a slave collar and go with you!"

Kincar shook his head and smiled a little crookedly. "Back to your wastelands, Kapal, and raise those men for a festing. Be sure I shall take care, and all we have learned from that guard is safely here." His hand went to his forehead, but he did not touch, remembering what was painted there.

The captive had talked, freely, in detail. Lord Dillan, the healer of sick minds, could have thoughts forth

117

when he wanted them. And all that other had re-counted was now Kincar's—the passwords for the fron-tier posts, customs, manners, minutiae that should take him safely in and out of U-Sippar, city of the lowlands.

Now, wishing no formal farewell, he headed Cim through the outer gate and rode out of the hold into the morning, down the cleft toward the openness of the lowlands. He did not once turn to see the fortress. As he had ridden out of Styr, so he now left this new se-curity to face a future that might be largely chance, but in a small part of his own making.

The promise of a fine morning did not last. But at the same time the wind that pulled at his cloak was surprisingly warm. And that was a warning to the weatherwise hunter. He could now be heading into one of the thaws of mid-cold season, when drenching rains blanketed the countryside, making traps of mire for the unwary—rains that turned in seconds, or so it seemed to unfortunates caught out in them, to icy sleet and freezing cold once more.

That map, supplied partly by Kapal and partly by their prisoner and memorized by Kincar, gave him a mental picture of a broad expanse of open plain. But between him and the first outposts of the plains civi-lization was a stretch of woodland. He had intended to ride south along the fringe of this to a river, then follow the bank of the stream seaward. But perhaps the forest would provide better shelter if the threatening storm broke before the day's end.

This Gorth had a different history than his own, even before the coming of the Star ships. That much they had learned in the past two days. In his Gorth the aliens landed upon a planet where the native race was just struggling out of barbaric tribal wanderings, a world without cities, without villages. The holds marked the first settlements of tribes influenced by the new knowledge of the outworld men. So their customs, laws, ways of life still held many elements of the nomads.

But this Gorth had already been well advanced from the primitive when the Star Lords had come to crush a rising civilization, hunt to extinction the native rulers who had built such fortresses as the hold, proscribe the old learning, the old religion. Where the Star men had striven to raise their own people, here they had reversed the process and attempted to reduce them to a dull level of slavery, not even equal to suard and mord or larng—for those were beasts, and their savage independence was reborn in each new generation.

Far from interbreeding with the natives, the outworlders here considered such a linkage of blood unspeakable, something obscene, so that Kapal found it extremely hard to accept as a fact that the hold men were partly of mixed-birth. But that might work to their advantage in another way, for the ranks of the Dark Ones here were exceedingly thin. A handful of births in a generation, and many deaths by assassination, by duels among themselves, kept the balance uneven.

Between each Dark One and his fellow there was only uneasy truce, and their guardsmen warred for a whim or an insult that had no meaning to the natives. Fear fattened upon night terrors, was not to be sated, even on battlefields or in burnt-out holds. Yet at the hint of an uprising—and in the beginning there had been many as Kapal testified—the mutual distrust and jealousy of the aliens was forgotten, and they combined forces to deal quick death. Of late years the few remaining sparks of freedom were to be found only in the wastes. And now the alien rulers were methodically stamping those out, one by one, as might men bringing boot soles down upon insects scurrying hopeless in the dust.

Cim kept to the ground-covering lope of his best journey pace. This wide stretch of snow-covered grassland was better going than the crooked trails of the hill country, and by mid-afternoon that same rising land was but a faint purplish line to the northeast. Still the warm wind blew steadily, and the snow melted under its touch, allowing yellow grass to show in ragged patches.

But the mount was not happy. He kept raising his head into the wind, snorting now and again. And twice he increased the length of his stride without any urging from his rider. They stopped for a breather on the crown of a small hillock, and Cim gave voice to a shuddering cry. Shadows moved in the far distance, and Kincar's hand went to his sword hilt. Not for the first time he regretted that he had had to leave his new bow behind. But those distant larngs had the elongated look of riderless mounts. A band of wild ones. There should be good trapping here come warm season. Loose Cim and a couple of other trained mounts to toll the herd into a pen— Why, they should be able to supply all the inhabitants of the hold with a second larng!

But would they still be in the hold at the coming of warm days? Foreboding swept away his hunter's enthusiasm. There had been little said during the immediate past of other gates, new Gorths to come, not since they had discovered the ills of this one. He was sure that the Star Lords were determined to do what they could to set matters right here before they essayed another passage through the ribbon rivers of cross time. And that did not mean that they would be peacefully hunting wild larngs.

Kincar twitched ear reins to call Cim to the duty at

hand, and the larng began his steady, distance-eating lope once again. His rider was certain that the thick line of the southwest marked the outer fringes of the forest he sought. And he was none too soon in that sighting, for the wind that wrapped around him now was as warm as a heating unit. The patches of snow were very few, and those grew visibly smaller.

Clouds now came rolling up the rose curve of the sky, driven by that too-balmy wind, clouds heavy and dark with rain, their sides as bulging as the water bags of wasteland travelers.

The first big drops spattered on his shoulders, caught in Cim's cold-season wool. Kincar pulled the flapping edges of his cloak about him and ducked his head, wishing he could pull it down between his shoulders as did a Lacker lizard. Cim shook his long neck, snorted disgustedly, and then fairly flew, an arrow pointed at the promise of shelter, still distant as it was.

They were well soaked before they made it under the trees. In leaf those would have been a good canopy. But now the rain drove among bare branches with a knife-edge force. And the warmth of the wind was gone; rather there was the bite of sleet. Where the moisture ran across bark, it was freezing into a clear casing of ice.

Somewhere they must find covering. Kincar's first annoyance became apprehension. The massing clouds had brought night in midafternoon. Blundering ahead might lose them in unmapped territory, but to halt in the icy flood was to invite freezing.

Kincar tried to keep Cim headed southwest, working a serpentine path that, he hoped, would bring them to the river. At any rate they must keep moving. He was on foot now, the reins looped about his wrist as he picked his way between tree trunks. And he must have unconsciously been following the old road for several minutes before he was aware of the faint traces left by men years before. The larger trees stood apart with only saplings of finger-size growth or low brush between. Then a tearing flash of blue-white lightning showed him smoothed blocks tilted up in the soil—a pavement here!

It appeared to run straight, and he turned into it, knowing that he dared no longer wander aimlessly in search of the river. At least a road went somewhere, and if he continued to grope his way along its traces, he would not commit the lost travelers' folly of moving in circles. A road tying the mountain district to the sea was a logical possibility. If he kept to it, perhaps he could even avoid some of the lowland outposts. And heartened by that, Kincar plowed along, towing the reluctant Cim, showered by the bushes he pushed between.

But very soon it was apparent that to find an ancient road for a guide was not enough. He had to have shelter, warmth, protection against the continuing fury of the storm. And Kincar began to search the gloom for a fallen tree against which he might erect a hunter's lean-to.

It was Cim who ended that. The larng squealed, gave a jerk of his head to bring Kincar's arm up at a painful angle before he could loose the reins. Then Cim reared, threatening Kincar with his clawed forefeet as he had been taught to savage a spearman in a fight. Caught off guard Kincar dropped the reins and stumbled back to avoid that lunge.

Free, Cim moved on, only dimly seen in the thickening gloom. He bobbed aside, struck away between two trees, and was gone before Kincar could catch up. Panting, floundering, the Gorthian hurried ahead, striving to keep the larng in sight. And from time to time he caught a glimpse of the lighter bulk of the mount.

Then Cim disappeared entirely. Half sobbing with frustration and rage, Kincar blundered on in the general direction in which he had last seen Cim, only to come up against a barrier with force enough to rebound into the prickly arms of a dagger-thorn bush.

His outstretched hands slid over stone glazed with the icy skim of the rain. A wall—a building—! Then those hands met nothing at all, and he had found an opening. He hurled himself forward and was out of the pelt of the storm, under a roof he could not see. Cim grunted, having found this shelter before him.

Kincar scuffed through a mass of leaves. Small branches cracked under his weight. Throwing aside his water-sodden cloak, he swept that debris together with his hands, before he brought out one of the mountaineer's clay boxes with its welcome coal.

At first he was too busy with nursing the small fire to life to inspect the structure into which Cim had led him. When the flames took hold, he looked about him for the supply of fuel—and found it woefully limited. Drifts of leaves, aged and a few rotten branches, none of promising size. He had brought in the smallest scraps before he noticed that another door opened into an inner chamber.

There was very little hope of finding any more wood in there, but he had to investigate. So Kincar crowded by Cim and stepped through that other doorway. The firelight did not reach past its threshold. But it was not the dark that made him hesitate—nor was it any visible portal.

When Kincar had passed the alien gates of the Star men, that talisman he had borne had taken fire from their energy, had been to him a burning brand to torment flesh. What he felt now was far different.

There was a gentle warmth—no stabbing heat. But, above and beyond that, a tingling, exhilarating feeling of aliveness, of senses brought to a higher pitch, a new depth of awareness. And with it a belief in the rightness of all this—

How long did he pause there, allowing that sensation of well-being to envelope him? Time had no meaning. Forgotten was the fire, the need for wood to feed it, the drum of the storm on the walls and roof that encased him. Kincar moved on into a dark that was at once warm, alive, knowing, wrapped in a welcoming security as a child is wrapped in a suard robe for sleeping by its mother.

There was no dark now. It hung before his physical eyes, but he walked with a truer sight. His fingers were swift and sure at the throat of his ring jerkin, loosening it, the other leather jacket underneath—his shirt. Then the Tie was in his hands. It glowed green-blue—with the sheen of fertile earth after the growing rains, of newly budded foliage.

Before him was an altar, a square table of stone, uncarved, fashioned with the same rugged simplicity as the shrine—a plain table of stone. But Kincar had seen its like before, though never had it been given to him to awaken what lay there, to summon what might be summoned.

A table of stone with three depressions, three small pockets hollowed in its surface. Its edge pressed lightly against his thighs now, bringing him to a stop. He did not have to stoop to use the Tie as it was meant to be used, a key to an unlocking that might occur only once in a man's life time and that changed him from that moment.

"Lor!" He called the Name clearly as he dropped the stone in the depression farthest to the left. "Loi!" Now that upon the right. "Lys!" The center. And the echo of the Three Names hung in the room, making music of a kind.

Were there now three glowing circles upon the wall? Three heads, three faces calm with a non-human serenity? His mind, coached by hoarded lore, the hundreds of legends, might be playing tricks and seeing things that his eyes in truth did not report.

Lor—He of the Three who gave strength to a man's body, force to his sword arm—a youth of beauty—

Loi—He who brought power, wisdom, strength of mind—a man of middle years with experience deep written on his quiet face—

Lys—She who gave gifts of the heart, who put children into women's arms, and friendship in the heart of one man toward another. Did a feminine face center between the other two?

What Kincar did see he could never describe. He was on his knees now, his arms on the altar encircling the depressions, with the Tie glowing bright and beautiful in the hollow that was Lys'. His head drooped forward so that the mark of shame he wore touched on the sacred stone, yet there was no deadening of the Tie glow.

And he slept. There were many dreams. He was taken on journeys and shown things that he would not recall when waking, and in his dreams he realized that and was sad. But there was a reason for that forgetting, and that he must accept also.

Perhaps it was because this was a deserted shrine, and the force pent there had not been released for untold time, that it poured forth now in a vast wave, engulfing him completely. He was changed, and in his dreams he knew that, shrank from it as earlier he had shrunk from the thought of his mixed blood.

It was morning. Gray stone walls, a flat table under

his head marked only by three small holes, in one of which rested a pebble with a chain through it. Kincar got to his feet and strode out without another glance at that dead room, for it was dead now. What had activated it the night before was gone—exhausted.

11

III-Chanced Meeting

That odd feeling of being cut off from the everyday world passed as Kincar stepped into the outer room of the shrine, just as his now dim memories of the night, of drawing upon the stored power of the Three, faded.

A blackened spot on the floor marked the fire he had started and abandoned hours ago. Cim hunched by the wall, his body heat, now that he was sheltered from the direct blasts of wind and wet, keeping him comfortable. He opened his top pair of eyes as Kincar crossed to him, moving his thick lips to suggest that a sharing out of supplies was now in order. But, though Kincar crumbled journeycake in his hands for Cim to lick away with every sign of healthy hunger, he himself ate only sparingly, more out of a sense of duty than from any inner demand.

The storm had deposited an encasing crystal film over all of the outer world. But the sun was up, and it was chill enough to promise no more unseasonable thaws. Such storms as yesterday's usually meant a space of fair weather to follow. However, the treacherous footing made Kincar decide against riding until they were out of the wood, and he picked a way with care back to the old road, Cim willing enough to follow him now.

It had been indeed a long time since any traveler had used this particular track. The forest was fast reclaiming it each season, uprooting, burrowing under, growing over. Only, those who had laid down these stones had been of the same clan of master builders as the men who had erected the hold, and they had not intended their handiwork to last only a short term of years. So the wild had not yet won.

Kincar guessed by his hunter's knowledge that he was now heading west, if not angling so much to the south as he had first planned. And since he was well concealed on this forgotten path, he determined to keep to it, believing it should bring him through the forest and into the open country about U-Sippar where he would have to travel with greater care.

It was late afternoon before the trees began to thin, and Cim pushed through the last screen of the forest into the country bordering the sea. In fact, this tongue of woodland had run out very close to the ocean's edge. But the port the road had once served was now a tumbled ruin of roofless buildings, battered by storms and time alike, with only slimed stone pillar heads to mark the wharves that had once extended into the brown-gray water.

Ruinous as it was, some life still clung to the place. A battered boat had been hauled well up on the shingle, turned bottom up with the scars of recent repairs on its rounded sides. And from a hut of ill-matched stones came a trickle of cooking-pot smoke.

As far as Kincar could see, there was no sign of any guard post, no suggestion that the mercenaries of the Dark Ones were in command here. Some fisherman, he surmised, had thrown up a shelter in the ancient port to net over grounds so long abandoned as to be worth searching once again.

He had allowed Cim free rein, and now the larng

continued to jog along the overgrown, soil-drifted road, winding a way among fallen debris. Kincar, running a knowledgeable eye over the buildings, their windows like the arched hollows given skulls for eyes, believed that the place had been despoiled in battle, a battle in which the inhabitants had fought without hope but with a grim determination, from house to house, wall to wall. Even the beating of many seasons' rains had not erased the stigma of fire. Splintered wood, powdering away, was riven with the blows that had beaten in doors and window coverings.

No wonder this had been abandoned after that day. Not many could have survived the sacking, and if the victor had not chosen to rebuild— Perhaps it had been decided to leave this as a warning and a threat for all time. In his own Gorth, traders had been handy men with a sword. They had to be; most trade roads led across wild lands. And while they did not spout challenges in every man's teeth, they drew blades in their own defense, forcing many an ambitious hold lord to a quick change of mind when he nursed some idea of an illegal tax because a trade route lay across his land. If this had been a town of traders, well then, the attackers had not had matters all their own way. And, Kincar, having no idea of the rights of the matter, but guessing much, was very pleased to think that true.

Seashore birds, scavengers of the tides, shrieked overhead. But, save for that thread of smoke and the boat, the shore was empty of any other sign of life. He did not know how far he was from U-Sippar, though that city being a port, he need only follow the shore line to find it. But—which way—north or south? And to journey on through the coming night was unwise. A lost traveler could, by rights, demand a lodging at the nearest dwelling in his Gorth—perhaps that custom held here.

Kincar headed Cim for the hut on the shore, the hint of food cooking being irresistible at the moment. A fisherman probably lived on the results of his labors. Kincar visualized some dishes, common enough on the shore no doubt, but luxuries in the mountains—shell fish for example—

Cim's clawed feet made no sound upon the sand, but possibly Kincar had been under observation for some time through one of the numerous cracks in the walls of the hut. Before he had time to dismount, or even hail the house, a man came out, shutting the wooden slab of door and taking a stand with his back against that portal that suggested he was prepared to defend it with his life.

In his right hand he held a weapon Kincar had seen only once, and then it had been a curiosity displayed by a trader. A straight shaft curved into a barbed point, resembling a giant fishhook—which in a manner it was. The trader had explained its use very graphically to the astonished men of Styr Holding. Hurled by the experienced in the proper manner, that hook could pierce armor and flesh, drag a mounted man down to where he could be stabbed or battered to death. And this fisherman handled the odd weapon as if he knew just what it could do.

Kincar looped Cim's reins over one arm and held up his empty hands in the old universal gesture of peace. But there was no peace mirrored in the other's set face, in his sullen eyes. His clothing, in spite of the harsh weather, was hardly better than a collection of stained and grimed rags, leaving the scabbed, cracked skin of arms and legs bare to elbow and knee, and the hollows beneath his cheek bones spelt starvation. If he got his living from the sea, it was not a good one.

"I come in peace," Kincar said slowly, with the authority he would have used speaking to a fieldman of Styr.

There was no answer, no indication that the other heard him. Only the hook turned slowly in those hands, the sullen eyes remained fixed on larng and rider—not as if they saw only an enemy—but also food!

Kincar sat very still. Perhaps this was no fisherman after all, but an outlaw driven to wild desperation. Such men were truly to be feared, since utter despair pushes a man over the border of sanity and he no longer knows danger to put a rein on his acts. Somehow Kincar was sure that if he drew his sword, if his hand traveled a fraction of an inch toward the hilt, that hook would swing—

His own eagerness—eagerness and weakness—undid the hook man. Kincar kneed Cim, and the larng gave the sidewise leap of a trained battle mount. He had read aright that twitch of the hands, that stiffening of the other's jaw muscles. The hook scraped across his shoulder, caught in his cloak. Then in a flash he had it and with one sharp jerk snaked its line through the other's hands with force enough to pull him off balance and face down in the sand. There was no sound from the disarmed man. He lay quiet for a moment and then, with more speed than Kincar would have credited to him, threw his body in a roll to bring him back against the door of the hut once again. He huddled there on his knees, his back braced against the salt-grayed wood, his hands on either side of the frame, plainly presenting his own body as a barrier against Kincar's entrance.

Kincar freed the hook from his torn cloak and let the ugly thing thud to the ground. It was well out of the reach of its owner, and he had taken a firm dislike to handling it. But he did not draw his sword.

"I come in peace," he said again firmly, with an em-

131

phasis he hoped would make sense to the man at the hut, penetrate his fog of desperation. Again he displayed empty hands. He could ride on, he supposed, find shelter elsewhere. But this other was in the proper frame of mind to dog his trail and perhaps ambush him along the shore. It was too late to keep on riding.

"Murren—?"

That call did not come from the man, but from inside the hut. And at it the guardian flattened himself still tighter, his head turning swiftly from side to side, in a vain attempt to hunt escape where none existed.

"Murren—?" The voice was thin, a ghost of the sea birds' mournful cries. Only some carrying quality in it raised it above the pound of the waves.

"I will do you no harm—" Kincar spoke again. He had forgotten that he wore the clothes of a guard, bore the false brand. He only knew that he could not ride on—not only because of his own safety, but also because there was need to find what lay behind this stubborn, hopeless defense of the hookman, and who called from behind that closed door.

"Murren—?" For the third time that cry. And now something more, a thud ringing hollow against the worn wood, as if one within beat for his freedom. "Murren—dead?" The voice soared close to hysteria, and for the first time the man without appeared to hear. He flattened his cheek against the wood and uttered a queer hoarse call of his own, like a beast's plaint.

"Out—Murren—!" the voice demanded; the beat on the door grew louder. "Murren, let me out!"

But the man held his position stubbornly, hunching his shoulders against the slab as if the disobedience of that order was in itself a source of pain. Kincar flicked the reins, and Cim advanced a step or two. The man shrank, his snarling face upturned, his eyes wild. He must have recognized a larng trained in battle savaging, be expecting those clawed forefeet to rake him down, yet he held to his post.

He could guard the door, but he could not contain the whole hut. There came the sound of splintering wood, and the man leaped to his feet. Too late, for a second figure wavered around the corner of the hut. Its clothing was as tattered as that of its guard, but there was a difference between them.

The man who had fought to protect the hut was a thick-featured, stocky individual of the fieldman breed. He might be a groom of larngs, a guardsman in some hold, an under officer even. But he was no war chief nor hold heir.

The newcomer was of another class—wholly Gorthian, of noble blood as far as Kincar could see, and no beaten slave. He was plainly at the end of his strength as he reeled along, with one hand on the hut wall to support himself. The youthful face raised to Kincar was delicate of feature, wan and drawn, but his shoulders were squared as if they were accustomed to the weight of a scale shirt.

He came to stand by his man, and they both fronted Kincar, weaponless but in a united defiance. The young man flung back his touseled head to speak.

"You have us, Hand. Call up your men. If you expect us to beg for a quick death, you shall be disappointed. Murren has been left unable to plead—if he would— which he would not. And I am as voiceless in such matters as your knives have left him. Let the Lord Rud have his pleasure with us as he wishes. Not even the Dark Ones can hold off death forever!" What had begun in defiance ended in an overwhelming weariness.

"Believe me—I do not come from Lord Rud, nor do I ride as one of any tail of his." Kincar strove to put all the sincerity he could muster into that. "I am a traveler, seeking shelter for the night—"

"Who expects a Hand to speak with a straight tongue?" Weariness weighted each word. "Though how lies profit you, I cannot see. Take us and make an end!"

Murren put his hands on the boy's shoulders and endeavored to set him back, behind his own bulk. But the other resisted.

"This is the end, Murren. Whistle up your men, Hand of evil!"

Kincar dismounted, his empty hands before him. "I am not hunting you."

At last that got through to the boy. He slumped back against Murren, whose arm went about him in support.

"So you are not hunting us; you have not been sent out of U-Sippar to run us down. But then we shall be your favor gifts for Lord Rud. Collar and take us in, Hand, and you will have his good wishes."

Kincar made a move he hoped would allay a measure of their suspicion. He pulled a packet of journeycake and dried meat from Cim's bags and tossed it across the space between them. It struck against Murren's foot. The man stared down at it as if it were a bolt from one of the Star Lords' weapons. Then he released his hold upon the boy and scooped it up, bewildered at what he found within the wrappings.

Murren thrust a piece of the cake into the boy's hand, giving voice to his own avid hunger with a whimpering cry. They crammed the food into their mouths. Kincar was shaken. The captives he had helped to free on the road had been, with the exception of Kapal, so sunk in their misery that they had hardly seemed human. He had tended them as he had tended Vorken when her wing had been singed, as he would have Cim. But these two were no slaves, apathetic, animal-like in their acceptance of degradation and pain.

"Who are you?" The boy had swallowed the cake, was now sucking on a stick of meat, eying Kincar as

Kincar might watch Lord Dillan engaged in some Star magic.

"I am Kincar of Styr—" It was better not to claim s'Rud here. And he must keep always in mind that this Gorth was not his Gorth. That Lord Rud, the tyrant of U-Sippar, was not the Lord Rud who had been his father.

"Styr—" The other shook his head slowly; the name plainly had no meaning for him.

"In the mountains." Kincar gave the setting of Styr, which probably did not exist in this Gorth.

The boy, still holding the meat stick as if he had forgotten he had it in hand, came forward to stand directly before Kincar. He studied the half-Gorthian's face with a searching that must have planted every line of it in his memory forever. Then with one finger he touched the mark, dropping his hand quickly.

"Who are you?" he asked again, and this time with a lord's authority.

"You have the truth—I am Kincar of Styr—out of the mountains."

"You dare much, mountain man!"

"How so?"

"To wear that and yet not wear it— Nay"—he shook his head—"I ask no questions. I wish to know nothing of what brought you here. We may be danger to each other."

"Who are you?" Kincar countered in his turn.

The other answered with a wry smile. "One who should never have been born. One who will speedily be naught, when Lord Rud finds me, as he must—for we are close to the end of our wayfaring, Murren and I. I have no name, Kincar of Styr, and you had best forget that our paths ever crossed. Unless you choose to win a goodly welcome at U-Sippar by taking me there—"

"In the meantime," Kincar said with deliberate

lightness of tone, "will you grant me shelter this night?"

If the boy was coming to accept him—if not as a friend, at least only a minor menace—Murren was not so disposed. He showed his teeth in a mord's hunger grin as Kincar came forward. Impulsively then the half-Gorthian did something that might have endangered his life, but it was the best example of good will he could think of. He went back, took up the hook, and skidded it across sand and gravel.

Murren was down in a flash, his fingers on its shaft. But as quickly the boy caught his arm.

"I know not how you are tossing your chance sticks in this game," he told Kincar, "but I accept that you will not act after the manner of those whose foul mark you wear. Murren—not this one!"

The older man mouthed a protest of yammered sound, and in that instant Kincar saw the real horror that had come upon him—he was tongueless! But the boy pulled him aside from the hut door.

"If you would claim shelter, stranger, it is yours. Silence can be exchanged for silence."

They had a fire, if they had no food, and in the hut there was a measure of warmth, walls against the night wind. Kincar tethered Cim nearby and gave the larng rations, Murren, ever at his side, turning the hook in his hands, kept only from its use by the influence the boy held over him. When they were all three inside, he stationed himself before the door, his sullen, very watchful eyes daring Kincar to a false move.

But the half-Gorthian was very content to settle down by the driftwood fire, hoping in time to gain some scraps of information from his chance-met companions. If they were outlaws of the coastlands, as the boy's talk of Lord Rud made it clear that they were, then they knew U-Sippar and could set him on the trail for that city. But to ask questions without raising suspicions was a delicate problem.

He was no student of men's minds. It needed the skill of Lord Dillan or the Lady Asgar to allay others' fears and make them talk freely. And there was very little time in which to work. Oddly it was the boy who gave him a good opening.

"You ride to U-Sippar?"

"Aye—"

The boy laughed. "You could not be coming from there. The search for us is up. Watch how you walk—or rather how you ride—man from Styr. Lord Rud's mords hunger, and they are appeased by those who cannot give good account of their activities."

"Even those wearing this?" His hand arose to his forehead.

"Now perhaps those wearing that. A secret was broke in U-Sippar." His lips twisted again in that smile that was no smile. "Though all its parts were smashed, as a man brings down his boot upon a soil-crawler, yet Lord Rud is not certain that is so. He will question all and everything for many days and nights to come. Think three times before you ride to that city without a tight tale, Kincar."

Had he accented that word "three"? Kincar took a chance. He spread out his hand in the glow of the fire, the red gleam making plain the movements of his fingers as they shaped a certain sign.

The boy said nothing—he might not understand. His features were well schooled, and he sat quietly for what seemed a long period of time. Then his own right hand went up in the proper answer.

"More than ever, it is well that you keep from U-Sippar!"

But already all warnings were too late. Cim did not have Vorken's superlative sight, but he had keen senses, superior to those of men. Now outside he shrilled a challenge to another male larng. The three jumped to their feet.

"This was an ill-chanced meeting, man from Styr,"said the youth. "You have been caught with us. But you can still save yourself—" He waited tensely, and Kincar grasped his meaning.

To claim these two as his captives would be his passport to favor. Instead he drew his dagger from his belt and tossed it to the unarmed boy, who caught it out of the air with a skilled hand.

"We shall see ill-chanced for whom!" Kincar returned.

12

A Meeting with Lord Rud

To Kincar there was no sense in remaining inside the hut, to be poked out of hiding as a cau-rat would be poked from its nest by a boy. Sword play needed space. But he had to thrust Murren out of the way at the door, and the boy needs must scuffle to follow him. The tongueless man was still making his protesting yammer as they came out into the twilight.

That fading light was yet bright enough to show that indeed their luck had run out. A ring of mounted men was closing in about the hut, and every other one of them balanced a lance ready to use. On Cim Kincar might have fought his way free. His larng was trained and strong enough to override these scrubby animals. But it never occurred to Kincar at that moment to desert the other two.

Only Murren was alert to such a possibility, proving himself more warrior than fieldman. It was he who sprang onto Cim's bare back and then leaned down to swing at the boy. His fist connected with the other's jaw, and the slight young body went limp. Murren got his master across his knees and drove Cim inland, swinging his hook as he charged against the wall of riders. And the very ferocity of his attack disconcerted the enemy as much as it astounded Kincar.

The hook rose and fell, and a stunned man tumbled from his larng, making a break in the wing. Murren used it, Cim leaping through like a hunted suard. Some of the party went after him at the shouted orders of their officer.

But the four or five who remained headed for Kincar, who set his back to the hut wall and waited tensely. Could he bluff it out—say that Murren and the boy had been his prisoners and had escaped? But the facts were too plain. Murren had been armed and Cim had been there for his use.

Lances against sword. It was an unequal contest at the best. He held his cloak ready to entangle a lance point. Had the encounter only come at night, he might have had a thin chance of escape under cover of the dark. But they were between him and the sea—no hope of swimming out—and there was a long open stretch of flat shore before one came to the nearest ruins of the old town. However, surrender without a fight was not to be thought of.

That was what they wanted. The nearest warrior hailed him.

"Put down your sword, stranger! The peace of the Gods between us—"

Not the peace of the Gods. The false gods. And any peace of their offering meant nothing. Kincar made no answer.

"Ride him down!" came a growl from the nearest lancer.

"Not so!" someone objected. "Lord Rud must have speech with any man found in the company of—" The other speaker bit off his words as if fearing an indiscretion. "Take him prisoner if you do not wish the Lord to overlook *you,* lackwit!"

They came at him from three sides. Kincar threw the cloak, shore away one lance point with his sword.

140

Then a larng reared to bring down its raking claws. He flung himself sideways and went down on one knee. Before he could recover, a lance butt was driven against his back with force enough to burst the air from his lungs and carry him down into the sand. They were all over him in an instant, grinding his face into the shingle as they whipped his arms behind him and locked his wrists together. Then they allowed him to lie there for a space, choking and gasping, while they held consultation over him.

For the time being Kincar was occupied with the suddenly difficult job of breathing. And he had not yet given over gasping when he was raised and flung roughly face down over the withers of a sweating larng.

It was a cold ride through the night, for Kincar had no cloak. It seemed that the riders were so well acquainted with the route that they dared travel it in darkness. Or else they were in such a well-founded fear of their overlord that it was worth the risk to carry him a quick report. However, a headdown journey was not an inducement to logical thinking or the forming of future plans. Kincar was only semiconscious at the end of that ride. When he was tumbled from the larng, he was as limp as a pair of saddlebags.

Dull pain reached through the general fog as a boot was planted in his ribs to turn him over. As he lay sprawled on his back, a light flashed blindingly into his eyes.

"—is he?"

"—bears the mark—"

"Whose man?"

Fragments of questions that had very little meaning. And then one order to bring action: "Put him in the cells and then report. If he was with the young one, Lord Rud must know it."

They did not try to get him to his feet. Fingers were

laced in his armpits, and he was dragged across a stone pavement, bumped downstairs. The fetid smell of damp underground closed about him along with a deeper darkness. Then he was shoved backwards so that he rolled down a few more steps. There was the slam of a door, and light was totally gone.

He had come to rest in an awkward position, legs higher than his head, and now he tried to wriggle backwards on a level surface until his feet slipped from the stairs. He was bruised, still groggy from the ride, numb with cold. But he had suffered no real hurt, and he was aroused enough to think rationally once more.

They had mentioned Lord Rud, so it followed that he must now be in some fortress of U-Sippar. And he had entered under the worst possible disadvantage—captured while companying with fugitives hunted by the district's ruler. They had noted his brand but had not marked its falsity, so he still had a faint chance to pass himself off as a man following some lord living at a distance. It was a very slender hope, but it was all he had left, and now Kincar made himself go over his story, testing its weakest points.

When that story had first been concocted back in the hold, they had never expected him to face one of the Dark Ones in person. His general instructions had been to enter U-Sippar as an unattached Hand seeking employment, but with enough loot in his pouch to keep him for a space before he had to take service. He was to keep away from the fortress, from the guards on duty there. And here he was in the very heart of the place to be most shunned.

Supposing that Lord Rud—this Lord Rud—was gifted as Lord Dillan with the power of acting upon men's minds. Or if he was not so himself, he could summon those who were. For the first time a new idea broke. If in this Gorth there was a Lord Rud, might

142

there not also be a Lord Dillan? What would it be like to confront a Lord Dillan who was different? That thought spun slowly through Kincar's mind.

Now, he told himself, he had only to remember that these Star Lords were not those he knew, that he must not be misled by resemblance. And he had as yet to see the proof of Lord Dillan's statement that men could have their counterparts in other worlds.

Time in the dark was not a matter of minutes and hours. It was a thing of cold, and growing hunger, and cramp in his pinioned arms, aches in his bruised body. He squirmed across the floor until his shoulders met a wall, and then, with infinite expenditure of energy, he was able to rise to his feet. Now by movement he could fight the cold, be in better shape to meet the ordeal that no doubt awaited him.

Using the wall as a guide he encircled the chamber. It was bare of any form of furnishing save in one corner where he padded over a heap of musty straw, perhaps the bedding of those unfortunates who had preceded him in its occupancy. He came to the stairs again. And for want of a better seat huddled there until the chill from the stone drove him up again.

How many times he circled, rested, and then circled again, Kincar did not try to count. But he was seated when he felt a vibration in the stone heralding the coming of his jailors. He was up and facing the door when that portal crashed back against the wall, and light flared at him from above, blinding him once more.

"Up on your feet, are you, dragtail?" demanded a voice with that sort of hearty humor that is more sinister than a curse. "Have him forth, you stumble feet, and let his betters see if he's ripe for the skinning—!"

Figures plunged out of the source of the light, hands fastened on him, shoulder and elbow, and he was propelled up the stairs and out into a stone-walled corridor. More stairs, then the light of a fair day, as they issued into a courtyard.

The men who hustled him along were guardsmen of the common sort, with flat, brutal faces, the spark of intelligence low behind their uncaring eyes. Their officer was a huge man. Kincar almost believed him of off-world breed until he saw the Gorthian features and the devil mark between his eyes. He grinned, showing tooth gaps, leaning over Kincar until his foul breath was thick in the younger man's nostrils. One big hand dug deep in Kincar's hair, pulling his head back at a painful angle.

"The mark right enough," remarked the giant. "But you'll find that will not save you here, youngling."

"Do we pin him, Sood?" inquired one of the guards.

The giant loosed his grasp on Kincar and slapped his open palm across the questioner's face, rocking him so that he stumbled against the prisoner.

"Tighten your lip, dirt! He's pinned when Sood says pin and not before. But he'll cry for pinning before we get the irons to him, so he will! Nay, larng scrapings, he goes to the hall; you get him there! You know who is not ever pleased to be kept waiting!"

The man who had been slapped spat red. But he made no protest at his rough disciplining, not even the inarticulate one of a glare at Sood's back as the giant marched ahead. Kincar was pushed on across the courtyard and under a second archway into the living quarters that were officers' territory.

They shuffled under an arch of rough stone into another world. Here was no stone, no native cloth arras as were stretched across the walls of Styr's Hold to keep out cold-season drafts. On either hand the walls were smooth with the sheen of a sword blade. They might have been coated with metal. And over their pale gray

144

surfaces there was a constant dance and play of rainbow color, which appeared, until one focused steadily upon it, to form pictures in an endless and ever changing series of ghostly scenes.

It was totally unlike anything Kincar had ever seen or heard described, and he guessed it was born of the off-world magic of the Star Lords. But he kept his surprise under control. He must appear to be familiar with such if he would carry out his pose as the ex-retainer of another lord in search of a new master.

A curtain of shimmering stuff fronted them. Without any touch from his guards, it parted, drew back against each wall to allow them through. Now they had come into a wide room. Sun flooded it from the roof, filtering through an intricate patterned crystal, which threw more rainbows on the floor. Evenly spaced about were a number of doors, each veiled with the strange curtains, while in the center was a square pit, some benches beside it. On those nearest Kincar, two Gorthians sat stiffly. There was no ease in their manner. They might have been fieldman bidden to eat at a hold lord's table because of some whim of that lord, wary at what would chance should that whim change. They did not turn their heads to look as Sood and the others tramped in but kept their attention upon the man at the other end of the pit, as a novice swordsman watched a master-of-blades during a lesson.

Here Sood, too, was dwarfed for all his giant's brawn, made to dwindle in an odd fashion. He was no longer a roistering bully to be feared, but a servant attendant on a lord of power. He advanced no further than within a foot or two of the occupied benches and stood waiting to be noticed.

The lord of this fortress, he who held in a child's discomfort fighting men and who dwarfed Sood, lounged at ease on a couch removed from the Gorthians by the width of the pit. He was lying full length on the padded surface, his head supported by his crossed arms as he watched something below. And there was no mistaking *his* birthright. This man was of the Star breed.

Hitherto Kincar had seen the off-worlders only in their silver battle dress, simple clothing designed for hard usage. This man wore a robe of some light fabric under which every movement of his muscles was plainly visible. He was as massive as Lord Dillan, but the clean, fine lines of Dillan's body were here blurred as if someone had tried to copy him from the same mold but with no master touch. There was a curve to a jaw line that should be square and sharp, a rounded softness of lip and chin. His hair was the most alien—a dull dark red, thick and straight.

Kincar had time for that appraisal because the Dark Lord was intent upon the pit. Then there came a thin squeaking from that opening, and he laughed, levering up his head to see the better.

"Well done!" He might have been cheering on some warrior duelist. "I win again, Calpar!"

There was a duet of agreement from the two Gorthians. But they were still watching their lord rather than the pit. Now he looked up—to sight Sood's party.

"Ah, Sood—" His voice was rich, almost caressing, only Kincar felt a sensation of cold as if he had walked barebodied into an ice storm. Here was something he had never met before. He had known awe with Lord Dillan, and to a greater degree with the Lady Asgar. With Lord Bardon he had felt the admiration of a warrior in the train of a noted chief. But none had given him that daunting of spirit, that feeling of being less than a larng in their sight. From this man he did not even strike the interest he would give to Vorken—he was less than a well-trained beast.

But that realization was consumed by a growing

146

heat within him, a heat that flamed outward, as the heat of the Tie had eaten inward when it had been so cruelly activated by the Star Lords' magic. Perhaps the men of this Gorth had been beaten long ago into accepting that valuation of themselves—but he had not. Kincar fronted the Dark Lord straightly, striving to keep under control both his aversion and his defiance.

"What have we here, Sood—" The purr lapped across the pit.

"The one who was taken at the hideout of *those*, Lord."

"The one who aided in their escape, aye. Bring forward this hero—"

Kincar was shoved ahead, to the very lip of the pit. But those who pushed him remained a little to the rear, sheltering behind him from their ruler's attention.

"And who may you be?" The Lord addressed Kincar directly.

"I am from the mountains, Lord—Kincar of Styr who was lately Hand to Lord Seemon—" He had chosen the lord who had ruled the captured guard, and hoped it would prove a good choice.

"And why, my good Hand, did you leave the service of Lord Seemon?"

"There was a sword quarrel set upon me, Lord. I killed my man, but he had brothers who took blade oath to meet me one by one—"

Lord Rud laughed. "You are an unlucky man, are you not, Kincar of Styr? First you kill a man with brothers to be active in his favor and then you make a long journey only to meddle in what concerns you not, so you come to an ill fate in U-Sippar. Tell me, Kincar of Styr, why did you befriend those dirt-eaters you met upon the shore?"

"Lord, I knew nothing of them, save that they said they were flying also from a blood feud—"

147

"*They* said? Ah, but I think that one of them was incapable of saying much, or had he miraculously grown once more a certain important piece of his body which had been stricken from him?"

"The young man said it, Lord," Kincar corrected himself. He knew very well that Lord Rud was playing a game with him, that sooner or later the alien would give an order to finish him.

"So they were flying from blood vengeance were they? Apt enough. But they will discover that one does not fly from some kinds of vengeance. They are within my hand, even as these—"

He made a gesture at the pit, and for the first time Kincar looked down into it. What he saw was a Gorthian scene in miniature—a thread of stream, trees no higher than his tallest finger, clearings he could cover with his palm. Yet water ran, trees and grass grew, and other things moved. A suard the size of a flying beetle grazed on open land. And on a trampled bit of ground lay—

Kincar swallowed. Great was the Star magic—but this! He could not believe what his eyes reported. The inner men of the mountains were manikins, but what were these tiny things? Manlike in form, manlike in their deaths, but surely they were not, had never been living things! Then he knew that his astonishment had betrayed him, for Lord Rud was watching him closely.

"One could almost believe," his silky words came deliberately, "that you had never seen the 'little ones' before, Kincar of Styr. Yet it is in my own knowledge that Lord Seemon has a fine company of such and that pit wars are the leading amusement in his hold. How odd that one of his men should be so ignorant of them! Perhaps we should ask you again, and with greater persuasion, just who you are and what you do in U-Sippar, Kincar of Styr. Not only do you keep very ill company for a loyal Hand, but also your past seems hazy, and that will not do at all. Not at all—"

"Lord, not all the men who serve one of your greatness are admitted to the inner chambers." Kincar seized upon the only argument that might save him. "I was no chieftain, nor a captain, but a young warrior. What amused my betters was none of my affair."

"Your wits are quick enough, that is certain." Lord Rud yawned. "Quick-witted natives are good sport. Sood, we have a puzzle here—"

The giant quivered in his eagerness, as a mord quivers before being signaled to the hunt. "Aye, Lord, shall we have him forth to the pins?"

"Sood, Sood!" The other laughed. "Always impatient. Break a man and then expect answers from the bloody bits. No, Sood, here are quick wits and perhaps something else." Lord Rud paused. His eyes—hard, dark, and yet with a fire in their depths—raked over Kincar. "I wonder, now, I wonder. Could Seemon have made a mistake in the dark?" He chuckled softly, as if nourishing some amusing idea. "Not the pins, Sood—at least not yet. It is a wearying business, this living ever penned within walls. I need amusement. Remove this Kincar but keep him in good condition, excellent condition, Sood. I want him whole of body and mind when I summon him again. Meanwhile, Kincar of Styr, you had best examine your conscience, reckon up the number of times you have twisted the truth to your own profit, for we shall have another time for questions and then I shall have straight answers! Oh, aye, I shall have them, Kincar of Styr, for am I not a god?"

He had a breathing space, if a limited one. Kincar clung to that. Every hour so won was a small victory for him. He presented a problem to Lord Rud, and as long as he continued to interest the bored ruler, so long might he hope for a slender measure of safety.

But Kincar breathed easier when he was out of the rainbow-walled inner chambers into the open day. Sood did not return him to the foul underground cell where he had been pent on his arrival. Rather he was marched up a flight of stairs into a tower room, which, bare as it was, had a crude bed, a table, and a bench, and might have been the quarters of a very junior officer. They loosened his wrist bonds and slapped coarse provisions on the table before they left him. Rubbing his wrists and wincing at the pain of returning circulation in his blue, swollen hands, Kincar crossed to the window to look out upon U-Sippar.

13

Ordeal by Mord

Though he was viewing it from an unusual angle, looking down upon those roofs and towers instead of up, still U-Sippar presented the unreal aspect of some city visited in dreams, where the most commonplace is linked with the bizarre. Here were ancient stone buildings, the work of the native Gorthians who had reached for the stars with their towers and sharply slanted rooftrees before the stars came to them with such devastating results. And from that honest stone sprang other structures, excrescences frankly alien to this earth. There were not many of these, only enough to distort the general outline of U-Sippar into something faintly corrupt and debased.

The fortress was part of it, a monstrous hybrid crouched upon an artificial rise, so that its shadow moved menacingly across the packed houses below with the climbing and setting of the sun. Half of it was of the stone, the rest of it new. And that portion flashed metallic, cold, smooth, like a sword pointed to sky.

Kincar could count four—no—five similar structures in U-Sippar. They could not all be dwelling places of Lord Rud. But surely each housed some measure of Star magic. The one farthest from him was planted so that sea waves washed about its foot. Though there were ships in the harbor, anchored there for the cold season when no trained mariner attempted passage into the freakish winds, none were tied up near the tower, and what purpose it might serve was beyond Kincar's powers of speculation.

Having seen U-Sippar, or as much of that city as could be viewed through a window slit, he set about the more urgent business of seeking a way out, not only of that room, but of the fortress itself. Unless he could shrink to less than Vorken's size—and possess her wings into the bargain—he could not attempt that window. And a single testing told him that the door was secured from the outside. An examination of the bed made it plain that bare hands could not rip loose any part of it for an improvised weapon, and the same was true of table and bench. He had been stripped by his captors of his outer ring-sewn jerkin and his belt, so even the empty sheaths of his weapons were gone. And since he was no hero of the song-smith's creation, he could not blast his way out with a well-tried spell.

But at least he could eat. And coming back to the table Kincar did just that. The fare was coarse, rations such as were given to the rank and file of guardsmen. But it was not prison fare, and he finished it to the last crumb of soggy milt-bread, the last swallow of sour frangal juice. Then he threw himself on the bed and tried to prove his right to Lord Rud's charge of quick wits.

Lord Rud! Was this the man his father had been in that alternate Gorth? Strange— His hands folded over the comforting bulge of the Tie. Had a change in history also wrought a change in a man's nature, the way Lord Dillan insisted that it would? This Lord Rud could not be the man he had heard extolled in the hold. This ruler was corruption, evil power, fear and death; the odor of his character was an evil smell throughout his stronghold.

Kincar wondered what would happen if the truth were made plain to this Dark One. And in the same instant he knew that no act, no betrayal, would be more fatal. No matter what chanced with Kincar of Styr—as long as he could, he must lock lips and mind alike against telling what he knew.

Had Murren and the boy escaped? Cim was better than any of the larngs he had seen in the troop that had captured him. And Murren's desperate dash might just have broken through the circle with enough force to give them the necessary start, since Cim had had a period of rest and was fairly fresh, and the troop mounts were weary at the end of a long day. That escape had been wholly Murren's improvisation—the boy would not have deserted another to the Hands of Lord Rud, though, because he bore the mark he did, the fugitives might have believed Kincar was in no great danger. What was the crime held against those two? From the bits he could piece together, it was enough to stir up all U-Sippar. He wished that they could have been picked up earlier by men from the hold.

So, in place of planning, his thoughts drifted from place to place, until, at last, the needs of his body could no longer be denied and he slept, while outside the sky over U-Sippar darkened into night and it seemed that Kincar of Styr was forgotten by his guards.

He was aroused by a cry so familiar that he lay blinking at the roof overhead, hazy as to where he was, certain for the space of an instant or two that he lay on his pallet within Styr's walls. That shriek, ear-torturing, came from the hatchery on the watchtower, where Vorken was doubtless exerting her authority over some rebel. Vorken was ruler of the Styr hatchery; let any other mord challenge her at its peril.

Vorken! Kincar sat up as he remembered. Vorken was gone and Styr, too, was farther away than if the whole of Gorth's sea lay between him and its towers!

There was a square patch of sun on the floor of his prison. It must be hours late into the morning. And he had been visited during sleep, for a jug and a plate, both filled, stood on the table. Apparently, if Lord Rud had not yet made up his mind concerning Kincar's disposal, his men were still under orders to treat their captive well.

Kincar ate as a duty. There was no reason to believe that such coddling of a prisoner would continue, and he'd best take rations while they were still coming. It was again fare of the most common sort, but it was filling and designed to satisfy men who were ready for a spear-festing.

While he munched away, he twice more heard the challenge call of a mord. But his window gave him no sight of any. The hatchery might be at the crown of the same tower in which he was locked, but mords always sought the heights when they took wing. That cry set him to a restless pacing, and, as time passed with a bar of sun creeping from crack to crack across the rough slabs of the floor, his impatience grew.

There was no doubt at all the Lord Rud planned some unpleasantness for him. And, knowing so little of U-Sippar, of this fortress, there was very little he could do on his own behalf. He would be as a child in Sood's paws, and the giant would be very pleased for a chance to subdue him physically. As to matching wits—who could match wits with the Star men?

The shaft of sun crawled on, disappeared. Kincar was by the window again, studying his knife-edge view of the city, when the outer bar of the door was drawn. He faced Sood and the two who had brought him there the previous day.

"Have him out!" Sood bade his underlings with the loftiness of a Star Lord, or his own interpretation of such. And he stood aside sucking his teeth while the

154

other two roughly rebound Kincar's wrists and gave him a shove doorwards as a reminder to move.

When he would have passed Sood, the giant put out a hand and held him. Fingers bit into flesh and muscle as Sood pawed at him, as a man might examine a larng for sale. And from that grip there was no wrenching away.

"There's good meat on him," Sood remarked. "The sky devils will not pick bare bones after all."

His two followers laughed nervously, as if it were very necessary to keep their officer in a good humor. But neither of them ventured any comment upon Sood's observation.

They went down the stairs and crossed the court. As they went, the majority of the men in sight fell in behind. And they did not re-enter the inner section of the fortress but trudged on through another gate and down a road, past three encircling walls with watchtowers and ramparts.

U-Sippar's fortress had not been built in the center of the town but straddled the narrow neck of land that extended into the sea bay from the main continent. Apparently those who had first planned the city's defenses had had nothing to fear from the ocean, but wanted a sturdy barrier between their homes and the interior. Now the party went inland, from the fringes of the town to a wide stretch of open field.

There was snow here, but the drifts had been leveled by the wind. And it was open for the maneuvering of mounted troops or for the staging of a spectacle. Kincar suspected that it was to be the latter use now. There was a gathering of Gorthians about the edges of that expanse, with mounted guards to keep a large center portion free.

As the party with the prisoner approached from the road, there was another arrival. Out from the upper

155

parts of the fortress shot a flying thing. It had no wings, it was not living, but some magic kept it aloft, hovering more than a man's height—a Star Lord's height—overhead. It circled, and as it passed over the natives, they fell face down on the ground. Then it swept up to confront Kincar and his guards. Lord Rud sat in one of the seats upon it and in the other—

Kincar had been warned—but until that moment he had not truly believed! That was Lord Dillan! But not, he told himself fiercely, not the Lord Dillan of the hold. *This* world's Lord Dillan. If he had not been prepared, he would have betrayed himself in that moment. Lord Rud was smiling down at him, and that smile, gay, charming, was colder than the air in which their breath smoked blue.

"A fit object lesson, brother," Lord Rud said to his companion.

But Lord Dillan leaned forward in his seat to study Kincar with a searching intensity. He spoke, his deep voice a contrast to Lord Rud's.

"He is no Hand."

"He bears their mark—"

"Then it is no proper mark. You!" Lord Dillan spoke to Sood, at the same time tossing to the giant a small box he had taken from his belt pouch. "Use that upon a piece of cloth and see if you can rub away that mark."

Sood ripped loose an end of Kincar's shirt and, dipping it into the paste in the box, scrubbed away with vicious jabs at the mark on the prisoner's forehead. The brand sign, which had resisted the rain and withstood all inadvertent touching since the Lady Asgar had set it on him, yielded. Sood's astonishment became triumph, and Lord Dillan—this Lord Dillan—nodded in satisfaction.

"As I told you, brother, this is no man of ours. Best

keep him for questioning. If someone has dared to plant the mark, they will dare other things. And the fault which you hold against him is relatively minor. What if he was found in the company of escaping slaves—do not all outlaws tend to herd together, until we gather them up? Or was there something about these particular slaves?"

He was eying his fellow lord sharply. And there was a dull flush on Lord Rud's face. He flung up his head.

"You rule in Yarth, brother, I in U-Sippar. Nor did I ask you hither; this visit was of your own planning. In another man's lordship one does not ask questions concerning his dealing of justice. This is an outlaw, come into our land to seek out knowledge to aid that rabble which others seem unable to beat out of their mountain holes. I will deal with him so that there will be few willing to follow him. Sood, make ready!"

Under his control the flier bounded higher into the air, so that Lord Dillan must clutch at his seat to keep erect, and then swerved to one side to hover.

However, Kincar had no attention to spare for the actions of Lord Rud and his brother, for the guards were on him, stripping away his clothing. His jerkin was slashed so that it could be drawn off without unpinioning his arms, and the shirt ripped in shreds to follow. But the man who tore at that paused, his eyes round and questioning, and he drew back hastily.

Sood, too, had sighted the talisman on Kincar's breast. The big man stood, his mouth working curiously, as if he must suddenly have a double supply of air for laboring lungs, and a dull stain crept up his thick throat to darken his weathered cheeks. These men wore a brand that divorced them utterly from the Tie, but the awe of that talisman held them as much, if not more, than it would a true believer. Perhaps,

Kincar had a flash of insight then, perhaps it was because they had ritually denied all that the Tie represented that it now possessed the greater power over them.

The giant was tough-fibered, far more so than the man who had pulled off the last of Kincar's shirt, for that guard's retreat turned into panic flight. He threw the rag as he was holding from him as he ran blindly down the field.

His comrade was not quite so moved, though he took his hands from the prisoner—Kincar might have been a fire coal—and shuffled back, his terrified eyes watching the captive as if he expected the latter to assume some monstrous guise. And he cried out as Sood's hand came up slowly, his fingers reaching to pluck away that round stone.

Sood had his brand of courage. He had to have an extra measure of self-confidence to hold his leadership among the bullies of U-Sippar's fortress. It was not by size and weight of arm alone that he had won his under-officership in Lord Rud's service. Now he forced himself to a task not one Gorthian in a hundred—in a thousand—would have had the will power, the hardened fiber, to attempt. Wearing that mark, proclaiming himself so to be what he was, yet he was prepared to set hand upon the Tie. From a barracks bully he was growing to a far more dangerous man.

"By Lor, by Loi, by Lys," Kincar said, "think what you do, Sood."

The gentle warmth that had answered his invocation of the Names told him that the stone was alive. What it might do to a branded one he could not guess, for to his knowledge such a happening had never occurred in the Gorth of his birth.

There were oily drops gathering along the edge of Sood's helm; his mouth was twisted into a skull's grin of tortured resolve. His fingers came closer. About the two there was a great silence. The wind had died; there was not even the plop of a larng's foot in the snow. The men of U-Sippar were frozen by something other than the cold of the season.

Sood made his last effort. He clutched at the stone, tugging at it so Kincar was dragged forward, the chain cutting into his neck. But that chain did not break, and the stone fell back against Kincar's skin, a blot of searing fire, to cool instantly.

Rud's under-officer stood still, his hand outstretched, the fingers bent as if they still held the Tie. For a second longer than normal time he stood so; then, holding that hand before him, he began to roar with pain and the terror of a wounded beast, for the fingers were shriveled, blackened—it was no longer a human hand. Being Sood, he was moved to kill as he suffered. His left hand brought out a knife clumsily; he stabbed blindly with tears of pain blurring his sight.

The sting of a slash crossed Kincar's shoulder; then the point of the blade caught in the Tie. Sood screamed this time, a high, thin sound, too high and thin to issue naturally from that thick throat. The knife fell from a hand that could no longer hold it, and the giant swayed back and forth on his feet, shaking his head, his hands before him—the one shriveled and black, the other red as if scalded.

Wounded he might be, but the blind hatred of the thing—of the man who wore the thing—that had blasted him, possessed all his senses. Kincar, his hands bound so that he could move only stiffly, was forced into a weird circling dance as the giant lurched after him to accomplish by weight alone what he had not been able to do with steel. Sood might lack the use of his hands, but to his slighter opponent he was still formidable.

The fate of the giant must have bewildered the rest of the guard. None of them moved to interfere with the two on the field. Kincar was so intent upon keeping away from the other that he heard a whistle only as a distant sound without meaning.

But the answer to that whistle had a great deal of meaning for both circling men. Lord Rud, baffled by the happenings of the past moments, but in no mind to lose control, had chosen ruthlessly to sacrifice the crippled Sood in company with this captive who knew too much. Where it had been planned that one naked prisoner would be exposed to certain death, two men moved. But the death was already in the air, and it would strike. Perhaps it would be all to the good. Sood was something of a legend in U-Sippar and should he be struck by a supernatural vengeance and the tale of it spread, it would put the countryside aflame. Let him die quickly, by a familiar means, and all that went before could be forgotten.

Kincar had not understood his fate at the whistle, but seconds later he knew it well. There was no mistaking the cry of a mord sighting meat—alive and moving meat—but yet meat for a hungry belly. And he guessed the type of death to which he had been condemned. Had his arms been free, had he a sword in his hands, he could have delayed that death—for a short space. But he could not have kept it away long. Against one well-trained mord an armed man, providing he was mounted and had a cloak, had a bare chance. Against a full hatch of them, that mounted warrior was lost, picked to the bones before blood had time enough to flow to the ground.

Sood was deaf, blind, unheeding of everything but Kincar. All the pain and shock of his hurts had crystallized into the urge to kill. He moved ponderously with deadly purpose. But, because he tried to use his hands time and time again, Kincar managed to elude his hold. The giant cried aloud, a wordless noise that was half plaint from pain, half demented rage at his inability to come to grips with his prey.

Perhaps it was that sound that drew the mords to him first. By rights the scent of the blood welling from the cut on Kincar's shoulder should have brought them down upon the younger man. However, the rushing wings centered on Sood, and they struck.

The giant's cry welled into a roar once more as, still only half aware of his peril, he beat at the swarming flesh-eaters. First he tried only to brush them aside so that he might attack Kincar. Then some spark of self-preservation awoke, and he flailed his arms vainly, his face already a gory mask.

Kincar, backing away from that horror, caught his boot heel on a turf and went down. His fall attracted several of the wheeling mords, and they swooped upon him. Claws bit into his upper arm, a beak stabbed at his eyes, and he could not restrain the scream torn out by his repulsion and fear.

But that beak did not strike him; the claws were sharp but they did not open gashes. There was the hiss of an aroused and angry mord, and the one on his body struck upward with open bill at another come to dispute her perch.

"Vorken!"

She chirruped in answer to her name. Vorken who had sought her kind in the mating season had found them—in the fortress hatchery of U-Sippar! And, knowing Vorken, Kincar could also believe that during her stay there she had with the greatest possible speed assumed rulership of the perches. Now it was only necessary for Cim to come trotting onto the field to make this truly an adventure of a song-smith's devising.

Only it was not Cim who came to take him away

from the murderous, horrible heap of twisting, fighting mords. It was the flier of the Dark Lords. And the false Lord Dillan with his own hands dragged Kincar onto its platform before it flew back to the fortress.

14

The Place of Towers

There was the crackle of speech in the alien tongue of the Star Lords. Kincar, seemingly forgotten for the moment, pulled himself up against a pillar, while Vorken chuckled throatily and waddled in a half circle about his feet, very proud of herself.

The wrangle continued. Lord Rud sat on a bench spitting out angry answers to a stream of questions Lord Dillan shot at him as he paced up and down that end of the hall, sometimes bringing his hands together with a sharp clap to emphasize a point. At first Kincar was so bemused by the wonder of his own escape from a particularly grisly death that he did not speculate as to why he had been lifted from the field. Now, from the gestures, from the sullen attitude of Lord Rud, the aroused state of this Lord Dillan, he guessed that his rescue had been made against Rud's will.

And this was borne out as the false Lord Dillan came striding away from his brother to stand before Kincar, looking him up and down.

"You are a priest of demons, fellow?"

Kincar shook his head. "I have not followed the Threefold Way," he replied as he would in his own Gorth.

That face—he knew every line of it, had believed that he could recognize every expression its muscles could shape! Yet to look upon it and know that the man who wore it was not the one to whom he had given his allegiance was a mind-wrenching thing, much harder than he had imagined such a meeting could be.

"So—we have not yet stamped out *that* foolishness!" Lord Dillan whirled and shouted a stream of angry words at Lord Rud. The other did not register only sullen denial this time. He walked toward them alertly.

"This one is from the mountains," he said in the Gorthian speech. "Look closely, Dillan. Has he the appearance of a lowlander? Without a doubt a creeper from some one of those outlaw pockets, trying to spy upon his betters. He should have been left as mord food—"

"Mord food, you fool!" Lord Dillan's exasperation was so open that Kincar looked to see him strike the other. "After what he did to Sood in the face of all this city? We have gone to great trouble to rout out this pestilent worship. Do you not see that the tale of what happened out there is going to spread and grow with the telling? Within days we shall have secret altars sprouting up again, spells being mouthed against us, all the other things to tie rebels together! You cannot erase from a thousand minds the manner of Sood's death. No, this one must be handled by the council. We must have out of him every scrap of knowledge, and then he must be reduced to groveling slavery before the eyes of his own kind. Abject life, not a martyr's death—can't you see the sense of that? Or, Rud, is it—" His speech slipped once more into the off-world language, and brother glared blackly at brother.

"We shall take him ourselves," Dillan stated. "We want no more natives seeing what was not meant for their eyes, hearing things certainly not intended for their ears. Send a message that we are coming by flier—"

Lord Rud's jaw jutted forward. "You are mighty free with your orders in another man's hold, Dillan. Suppose I do not choose to leave U-Sippar at this moment. As you pointed out, that scene on the field will doubtless provide fuel for rebellion. And my place is here to stamp such fires to ashes before they can spread."

"Well enough. Remain and put out your fires, though if U-Sippar was under proper control, I should think there was no need for such careful wardenship." Lord Dillan smiled slyly. "I shall take the prisoner in for questioning—"

It was very plain that that was not to Lord Rud's taste either.

"He is my prisoner, taken by my men."

"True enough. But you did not assess his importance until it was driven home to you. And your reluctance now to turn him over to the authorities argues that you may have some hidden reason to wish him quickly dead." Lord Dillan fell to studying Kincar once more. "What is this great secret, fellow, for which your lips must be permanently sealed? I wonder—" His hand closed about Kincar's upper arm, bringing the younger man up to stand under a clear shaft of light. He eyed him with an intensity that had something deadly and malignant in it.

"The Great Law, Rud," Dillan spoke very softly. "I wonder how many times it has been broken and by whom among us. The Great Law— Usually the fruits of its breaking can be early detected. But perhaps now and again such cannot. Who are you, fellow?"

"Kincar of Styr—"

"Kincar of Styr," the other repeated. "Now that can mean anything at all. What is Styr, and where does it lie? Should it not rather be Kincar s'Rud?"

165

He had guessed the truth, but in the wrong way. Perhaps some shade of surprise in Kincar's eyes convinced his questioner he was on the right track, for Lord Dillan laughed softly.

"Another matter for the council to inquire into—"

Lord Rud's face was a mask of rage. "For that you shall answer to me, Dillan, even though we be brothers! He is not of my fathering, and you cannot pin law-breaking on me! I have enemies enough, perhaps of close kin"—he eyed his brother hotly—"who would be willing to set up a tool, well coached, to drag me into trouble by such a story. Look to yourself, Dillan, on the day, in that hour, when you bring such an accusation before the council!"

"In any event, he needs be shaken free of all information. And the sooner the better. It is to your own advantage, Rud, that he tells the full and complete truth before all of us. If he is not the fruit of law-breaking, let us be sure of that and speedily."

As if to draw his brother away from a dangerous line of investigation, Lord Rud asked, "But why did Sood suffer? Let us have a closer look at that thing he is wearing—"

He reached for the Tie. Kincar pulled back, the only defensive movement he could make. But before those fingers closed upon the stone, Lord Dillan had slapped down that questing hand.

"If you value your skin, you'll leave that alone!" he warned.

"Do you think that I'll be burnt as was Sood? Why— I'm no ignorant native—"

"Sood's fate was aggravated because he wore the mark," Lord Dillan explained almost absently. "But we have no inkling as to the power of these things or how they can be used against alien bodies. And until we do know more, it is wisest not to meddle. I have only seen

166

one before, and that was just for an instant before its destruction by the witch doctor who had been wearing it. We'd overrun his shrine at night and caught him unawares. We'll have plenty of time to deal with this—and its wearer—when we get them to the towers. And that is where we should go at once."

They were talking, Kincar thought bitterly, as if he had no identity or will of his own except as a possession of theirs—which, he was forced to admit bleakly, was at that moment the exact truth. The only concession his captors made to the fact that he was flesh and blood was to throw a cloak over his half-bare body after they had put him aboard the flier, to lie, bound wrist and ankle, by their feet.

Vorken had protested such handling, and, for an instant or two, it appeared that she would be destroyed for her impudence. Then the false Lord Dillan decided that her link with Kincar must be thoroughly explored. She was muffled in another cloak and bundled in beside Kincar, where her constant tries for freedom kept the improvised bag bumping up and down.

To fly through the air was a terrifying experience. Kincar had ranged the mountain heights since he had been large enough to keep his seat on a larng pad and follow Wurd hunting, in the years before the old lord of Styr had been reduced to level country riding and at last to his bed. And Wurd's acquaintance with sheer ledges, far drops, cliff edges had been wide. But to stand with one's boots planted on solid rock and look out upon nothingness was far different, Kincar discovered, than to rise into that nothingness knowing that under one was only a flat platform of no great thickness.

He fought his panic, that picture his imagination kept in the forepart of his mind of the platform dissolving, of his helpless body turning over and over as it fell to the ground below. How had the Star men been able to travel the sky and the depths of space? Or were they alien to this fear he knew? He wriggled about, but all he could see of the two were their feet. The Star Lords of his own Gorth had had no such fliers. However, they might well accept such traveling as natural.

There was a windbreak on the front of the platform, and he was lying behind the control seats. Yet the chill of that journey bit deep, and the cloak was but small protection. As the minutes passed, Kincar's panic subsided, and it seemed to him that from the Tie spread a gentle heat to banish the worst of the cold. He had been afraid on the field when the mord hatch had turned their attention to him, but that was an honest fear to be fully understood. Now he knew a queer apprehension, the same quiver of nerves and tenseness of muscles that a swordsman knows before the command to charge is given at a spear-festing. He tried to school himself with the knowledge that for him there would probably be no return from this flight.

Against Gorthian captivity a man could plan, foresee. But among the Star Lords what chance had he? There was but one thing—Sood's amazing experience with the Tie and this Lord Dillan's wariness of that same token. A slim advantage—perhaps. He had listened to talk in the mountain hold. There were unseen powers—"energies" the Lord Dillan he followed called them. Some of these energies had activated the between-worlds gates through which they had come into this Gorth. And during that passage the Tie had also proved to be a conductor of energy, as Kincar could prove by a scar he would carry until he passed into the Forest.

The Tie, in addition, might have its own "energies," which would be inimical to the aliens. That night in the forgotten shrine, the talisman had been recharged with the power native to it. It must carry a full supply.

If he only knew more of its potentialities! But he had had no desire to follow the Threefold Way, to train as a Man of Power—for he had understood that he could not have the Way and Styr together and his heart had lain with Styr. So all he had to guide him were the mystical invocations of any believer, the legends and half-whispers. Had he been adept with the Tie, what might he not have accomplished—what could he not do?

The flier swooped, and Kincar fought sickness from the resulting flare of panic. Was it falling, coming apart to crash them to the earth?

But the swift descent slowed. Walls flowed up to cut off the light. They might be dropping down the mouth of a well. The flier came to a stop with less force than that with which a foot is set upon the floor, and both Star men arose. They had reached their destination.

Lord Rud made no move toward the captive. It seemed that he disliked laying hand upon Kincar. But Lord Dillan pulled the half-Gorthian up, cut the thongs about his ankles and, surprisingly enough, those about his wrists also. His arms fell heavily to his sides, his hands swollen. Lord Dillan picked up the bag containing Vorken and thrust it at him. He caught it clumsily, making a silent resolve not to display any sign of the intense pain any movement of hands or arms cost him.

"You will walk quietly where you are told." Lord Dillan spoke with the exactitude of one giving orders to a slow-witted child. "For if you do not, you shall be burned with this force stick." He had taken from his belt a rod not unlike the one Kincar had used in suard-hunting. "It will not kill, but the pain will be worse than death by mord, and you shall never be free of it. Do you understand?"

Kincar nodded. He could believe that the Dark One meant exactly what he said and uttered no vain bluff.

Could he hope for a speedy death if he attempted flight? Would he flee if that were the end? As long as a man was alive, he could nourish hope, and Kincar had not yet reached the point where he would try for death as a hunter tries for an easy thrust at his prey. Carrying Vorken, he obediently followed Lord Rud out of the chamber where the flier rested, down a sideway, while behind tramped Lord Dillan, weapon in hand.

The living quarters of the fortress at U-Sippar had been of alien workmanship and materials. The narrow passage in which they now walked was as unlike that as *that* had been from the Gorthian architecture upon which it had been based. Here were no flitting rainbow colors, only an even sheen of gray, which, as he brushed against it, gave to Kincar the feel of metal. And the passage ended after a few feet in a stair ascending in a spiral, the steps no wider than a ladder's treads. Kincar grasped the guard rail, Vorken in the crook of his left arm. He kept his eyes resolutely on the legs of Lord Rud going up and up, refusing to yield to any temptation to look down into the dizzy well beneath them.

They passed through a series of levels from which ran other passages, emerging from the floor of such a level to climb again through its roof. Kincar could not even speculate upon the nature of the building in which so unusual a staircase formed the core. On the third such level Lord Rud stood away from the stair, turning into a side corridor, and Kincar went after him. So far they might have been in a deserted building. Though the noise of their climbing feet echoed hollowly up and down that well, there had been no other sound to break the quiet, no sign of any guardsman or servant on duty. And there was a queer, indefinable odor—not the dank emanation of the hold walls, of U-Sippar's fortress, but in its way as redolent of a remote past, of something long closed against the freshness of wind and cleansing sunlight.

The passage into which Rud had turned was hardly more than a good stride long. He set his palm flat upon a closed door, and under that touch it rolled back into the wall so that they might enter an odd chamber. It was a half circle, a curved wall ending in a straight one—the shape of a strung bow, the door being in the straight wall. Spaced at intervals along the curved surface were round windows covered with a clear substance strange to Kincar.

A padded bench ran along the wall under the level of the windows, and there was an equally padded covering on the floor and over the walls. Otherwise the room was bare of either inhabitants or furnishings. Lord Rud glanced around and then stepped aside to allow Kincar to enter. When the Gorthian had passed through the door, he went out and the portal closed, leaving Kincar alone.

He pulled loose the covering about Vorken and evaded the exasperated snap of her bill, loosing her on the bench where she waddled along with her queer rolling gait, her claws puncturing its padding and having to be pulled out laboriously at every step. Kincar knelt on the same surface to look from one of the windows.

No U-Sippar lay without. The structure he could survey was totally unlike anything he had seen on either Gorth. Beyond were several towers, not the square stone ones he had known all his life. Fashioned of metal, they caught the sun and reflected its beams in a blaze of fire. All were exactly alike, round with pointed tips that stood tall in the sky. Kincar surmised that a similar building harbored him. Linking all of them together—by pressing tight to the transparent pane he could just make them out—were a series of walls—walls thick enough to contain corridors or rooms. But those were of the native stone. Metal towers—pointed—

Kincar's swollen hands closed upon the edge of the window until he felt the pain of that grip. Not towers—no, not towers. Ships! The sky ships of the Star men—here forever earthbound, built into a weird fortress. He had heard them described too many times by men who had visited Terranna on his own Gorth not to recognize them. Was this the Terranna of this Gorth? It could be nothing less than the heart of the Dark Ones' holdings.

On his own Gorth those ships had gone forth again—out to the stars. Here that must be impossible. They had been anchored to the earth. They had rooted their ships, determined to possess Gorth for all time.

As he studied that strange mating of ship and stone, Kincar could spot no signs of life. Nothing moved along those walls, showed at any of the round ports that now served as windows. And there was a sense of long absence of tenantry about it all. A storehouse—Kincar could not have told why that particular thought took possession of him nor why the conviction grew that he was right. This must be a storehouse for the aliens. As that it would be well guarded, if not by warriors, then by the magic the Star men controlled. A race who flew through the air without wonder would have weapons mightier than any sword swung by a Hand to protect their secret place.

The age-old thirst that arises in any man at the thought of treasure tempted Kincar. This whole city, fortress, whatever it was, must be thinly populated. If he could get free of his present lodging and explore—! But the door was sealed tightly. Vorken hissed from the bench. She was uneasy in this closed room as she had never been in the hold. Kincar went from one window to another. Three merely showed him other aspects of the tower-ship building, but the other two gave him a view of the countryside.

There were no trees, but odd twisted rocks. Some, with a puff crown of snow, were vaguely familiar. He had certainly seen their like before. Then the vivid memory of their ride through the wasteland desert to the first gate returned. There were no signs of vegetation here, unless its withered remnants lay under the snow. But in the distance was the bluish line of hills, the mark of mountains. And seeing those, Kincar's hopes rose illogically.

Vorken's head bumped against him. She raised a forefoot to scrape his arm and draw his attention. Though none of his race had ever believed the mords lacked intelligence, it was generally conceded that their mental mazes were so alien to that of mankind that communication between the two species was strictly limited to the recognition of a few simple suggestions, mostly dealing with food and hunting. But it was plain that now Vorken was trying to convey something in her own way. And he did what otherwise he would have hesitated to try, since mords were notoriously averse to handling. He sat down on the bench and lifted her to his knees.

She complained with a hiss or two. Then she squatted, her red eyes fastened upon his as if she would force upon him some message. She flapped her wings and mouthed the shrill whistle she gave when sighting game.

Kincar's preoccupation with Vorken was broken by the sudden heat on his breast. The Tie was glowing. Somewhere within the ship-tower an energy was being loosed to which that highly sensitive talisman responded. He hesitated. Should he take it off lest he risk a bad burn and incapacitate himself—or should he continue to wear it?

To his overwhelming surprise, Vorken stretched her skinny neck and butted her head against him, directly over the Tie, before he could fend her away. She pressed tightly to it, lifting her claws in warning when he would have moved her, giving voice to the guttural battle croaks of her kind.

The warmth of the Tie increased as the mord pressed it tightly against him. But that did not appear to disconcert Vorken. Her battle cries stopped. Now she chuckled, the little sound she made when she was very content with her world. And Kincar himself felt relaxed, confident, fast losing his awe of both surroundings and captors.

15

Trial of Strengths

That sense of well-being persisted. Vorken's beak gaped in a yawn. Her eyes closed as she huddled close, her grotesque head still resting against him. But Kincar felt far from sleepy. Instead he was alert mentally and physically, as he had never been before that he could remember. The feeling that there was no task beyond his accomplishing grew. Was this how the full blood of the Star breed lived? It must be! This supreme confidence in one's self, the certainty that no difficulty was too great—

Kincar laughed softly. And something in that sound struck below the surface of his present well-being, brought a tinge of doubt. Perhaps because of the Tie he was doubly alert to any hint of danger. Did that emotion, the self-confidence, stem from the energy in the talisman, or was it more magic of an alien sort? It would be very easy to work upon a man's mind—if you had the Star resources—to give him an elevated belief in his own powers until he was rendered careless. So very easy.

There was one way of testing that. Kincar lifted the Tie by its chain, slipped the chain over his head, and put down the stone at a short distance from him on the bench. The warmth on his flesh was gone. Vorken stirred. Her head arose as she regarded Kincar with an open question. But he was too preoccupied to watch the mord.

Pressing in upon him, with the force of a blow from a giant's fist, was an overwhelming and devastating panic, a fear so abject and complete that he dared not move, could only get air into his cramped and aching lungs in short gasps. His hands were wet and slippery, his mouth dry, a sickness ate him up inwardly. In all his life he had never known such terror. It was crushing all identity from him, turning him from Kincar into a mindless, whimpering *thing!* And the worst of it was that he could not put name to the reason for that fear. It was inside him, not from without, and it was filling all of his burnt-out body shell—

Vorken squalled, a scream that tore at his ears. Then the mord struck, raking him with her claws. The pain of her attack broke the spell momentarily. He made a supreme effort, and by its chain drew the Tie back into his hands. In those sweating palms he cupped it tight as Vorken ripped at him. But once he had it, the panic was gone, and when the chain was again over his head, the Tie resting in its old place, he sat weak and shaken, but whole and sane once more—so whole and sane he could not quite believe in what had struck him as viciously as the mord.

Blood trickled from the scratches Vorken had given him. Luckily she had not torn deeply. Now she crouched once more on his knees, turning her head from side to side, giving voice to a whimpering complaint as one of her punishing forefeet raised to the Tie. It was that talisman that had saved them both from utter madness—the why and wherefore of that deliverance being more than Kincar could understand. He could only accept rescue with gratitude.

Kincar had left Styr with no more training than any

youth who could confidently aspire to the lordship of a holding, and a small, mountain holding at that. He had ridden away under the shock of the abrupt revelation of his half-blood, unable to quite accept that heritage. Wurd's secret gift of the Tie, with all that meant, had been an additional push along a new path of life. His painful experience at the gates, and his acceptance thereafter by Lord Dillan and the Lady Asgar as one who had rightful guardianship of a power they respected, had tempered him yet more. Perhaps his volunteering for the expedition into the lowlands had been born of a spirit of adventure, rooted in the quality that sent any young warrior to a spear-festing. But with it had gone the knowledge that he alone of the hold was fitted for that journey—

What had happened that night in the forest shrine he did not understand. He was no adept to be able to recall the work of the Three. But now he believed that he had ridden away from there subtly altered from the Kincar who had taken shelter. This last ordeal might be another milepost on his road. He would not be as the Star Lords, nor as the ruler of Styr that he might have been had Jord not taken from him that future—but a person he was not yet able to recognize.

Kincar was sure he was no mystic, no seeker of visions, or wielder of strange powers. What he *was*—now—he did not know. Nor did he have the time to become acquainted. It was better to accept the ancient beliefs of his people—his mother's people—and think that he was a tool, mayhap a weapon, for the use of the Three, that all he did was in Their service.

There was a security in that belief. And just now more than anything else he desired security, to trust in something outside his own shaken mind and body.

He had been right in his surmise that he would be allowed scant time for self-examination. The door of the chamber rolled back into the wall. Vorken hissed, flapped her wings, and would have taken to the air in attack had not Kincar, fearing for her life, made a hasty grab for her feet.

Lord Dillan stood there. He did not speak at once, but, though he did not display surprise by any sign readable to Kincar, the latter thought his alertness astonished the other.

"Slave—" The harsh grate of the Star Lord's voice was meant to sting, as the whips of the Hands had stung their miserable captives.

Kincar stared as steadily back. Did the Dark One expect from him a cringing plea for nonexistent mercy?

Now the wand of power was in Dillan's hands as he spoke again.

"We have underestimated you it seems, fellow!"

"It appears that you did, Lord." The words came to Kincar as if someone else who stood apart and watched this scene selected them for his saying.

"Rud's offspring in truth!" Lord Dillan laughed. "Only our own kin could stand up against a conditioner set at that level. Let him try to deny this to the council. Come—you!"

He gestured and Kincar went. Vorken had struggled free of his grip and now balanced on his shoulder, a process made painful by her claws. Yet he was glad to have her with him, a steadying reminder of that other Gorth where a man could not be so beset by magic.

"Up!" The single word set him climbing once more, up the ladder spiral of the stairway. On the next level they came upon something he had not sighted from the windows. Connecting one ship with another, strung far above the ground, was an aerial bridge—temporary, Kincar judged, for so light-weight a creation could not survive the first real windstorm.

But frail as it was, it was also now their road. Kincar

178

clung with his full strength to the hand rope, some of the fear he had known on the flying platform sweeping back. To stop at all, he guessed, would be fatal. So he made the crossing, step by step, his attention all for the port door ahead.

He was within a foot of two of that door when he remembered Vorken. He had no way of escape—that he could see now—from the towers, not with the armed Lord Dillan ready to blast him. But perhaps Vorken could be saved. Still holding to the guide rope with his left hand, he half turned, flicking out with his cloak, at the same time giving the hunter's call for a sky search.

Was it by luck alone that the edge of the cloak entangled with the Star weapon? He had been well trained in the swordsman's art of using the enveloping fabric to bewilder and disarm an opponent, but he had never attempted such a throw under these adverse circumstances. Skill or luck, he engaged the rod until Vorken was up and away, rising cannily not in her usual spirals but headed in an arrow's flight for the distant hills.

Oddly enough, Lord Dillan made no effort at retaliation. He loosened the cloak, and it went flapping down into the chasm below them, where Kincar dared not look. He had not been lucky or skillful enough to have dragged the weapon from the other, and now it was centered upon him.

"Go on," Lord Dillan ordered, and Kincar, sure of Vorken's escape and treasuring that small triumph, went ahead, passing through the port into the second of the Star ship towers.

Two more of the Star Lords awaited him there—but neither were doubles of those he had known in the hold. To be faced by a Lord Frans, a Lord Bardon, a Lord Jon who were not what they appeared would have added

179

to his burden at that moment. These men were all younger than Lord Dillan, if he could judge the age of the Star breed rightly, and both looked soft, lacking that alertness of mind and body his captor possessed— traces of which Lord Rud had displayed. They had that inborn arrogance that comes not from the authority of a man who has rightfully held leadership over his fellows through innate traits of character, but that which is based instead upon never having one's will disputed, and having absolute power over other intelligent beings by birthright alone.

Neither concealed his amazement at Kincar, one asking Lord Dillan a question in their tongue. He snapped an impatient answer and motioned them on.

"Follow!" he told Kincar tersely.

They were about to descend another of the spiral stairways. Descend it! A glimmer of a plan was born— a fantastic plan—perhaps so fantastic that it would work! Success would depend upon how quickly Kincar could move, whether he would be able to take his guards by surprise. He did not think too highly of the newcomers, but Lord Dillan was another matter. However, the cloak trick had worked against him. Kincar could only try, desperate as the plan was. And, making his first move, he clutched at the hand rail of the stair. What he intended might well burn the flesh from his hands. He must have some protection for them— He was bare to the waist; there was no way to tear any strips from his hide breeches. If he only had the cloak again!

One young Star Lord was already passing through the first of the well openings. He was the only barrier between Kincar and the realization of his plan. And he was wearing not the tight weather suit of Lord Dillan but a loose shirt of some light material.

Kincar started down the ladder with a meekness he

trusted would be disarming. The steps were so narrow, the incline so steep that he hoped Lord Dillan would have to give a measure of his attention to his own going and so might be a second or so late in attacking when the prisoner moved.

The young lord was disappearing into the well at the next level now and Lord Dillan was waist-deep in the first, Kincar on the stair between them. The Gorthian threw himself forward, his weight on his hands. To the watcher it might seem he had missed a step. His foot swung out and caught the young lord on the side of the head. The other gave a choked cry and caught at the floor. It was that instinctive move to save himself that aided Kincar. He landed beside the alien and tore at his shirt, the thin stuff coming away in his hand. He pushed through the well opening, pulling over the half-conscious man to block it after him, and slid down the spiral, with only his hands on the rail as support.

He whirled about, wondering if he *could* brake his descent now. There were shouts behind, perhaps calls for help, and the clatter of boots. Friction charred the cloth under his hands, pain bit at his palms, but he held on. Two more levels, three; there was a regular din behind him now. Beneath him, two levels ahead, was solid floor, and he made ready as best he could to meet it. With dim memories of how he had taken falls in his first days of riding, he willed his muscles to go limp, tried to ball together, and prayed against the horror of broken bones.

There was blackness, but even in the semiconscious state he still strove for escape. When he was again truly aware of his surroundings, he crawled on smarting hands and aching knees down a narrow corridor.

Praise be to the Three, he had come through that landing unbroken, though his body ached with bruises.

Wincing at sharp stabs, Kincar got to his feet and lurched on, only wanting now to put as much distance between himself and the noise as he could.

The walls about him changed as he stumbled over a high step. They were stone, not metal, now. He must be within one of the walls that tied together the ship-towers—far nearer ground level. Surely here he could find a door to the outer world.

Though he did not know it until afterwards, Kincar was perhaps the first prisoner within that maze who was in command of his mind and body, unbroken by the conditioner. To the men who hunted him, he was an unknown quantity they were not prepared to handle. They did not give him credit for either the initiative or the speed and energy he was able to muster.

The stone-walled corridor wove on with no breaks of either windows or doors. He sped along it at the best pace he could keep, nursing his scorched hands against the Tie, for it seemed to him that there was some healing virtue in the talisman. At least it drew away the worst of the pain.

To his dismay Kincar came to a second of the ridge steps, marking the entrance to another ship-tower. But there was no turning back, and, with all the chambers that must exist in the ships, he could either find a hiding place or access through a port window to the top of a connecting wall. The dim light that radiated from both walls of stone and of metal showed him another spiral stairway. He made a complete circuit below. Two doors, both fast closed, and neither would open. He dared not linger there. Necessity sent him climbing.

The first level gave upon more doors all closed, all resisting his efforts to force them. Another level, the same story. He leaned, gasping, against the hand rail, fearing that he had been driven into a trap with the Dark Ones able to pick him up at their leisure.

The third level, and as his head arose through the well, he could have shouted aloud his cry of triumph— for here a door gaped. In his eagerness he stumbled and went to one knee. And in that moment he heard the unmistakable pound of feet below.

He fell rather than sprang through the door. Then he set his hand flat against it as he had seen Lord Dillan do. It moved! It fell into place behind him! He could see no way of locking it, but the very fact that there was now a closed door between him and the stairwell gave a ghost of safety.

The corridor before him was a short one, and he burst into a small, round room. The walls rose up to the open sky— He had seen it—or its like before—for here was berthed a flier like the one that had brought him here.

He was trapped. There was no climbing the smooth walls of the well that held the flier. Soon—any moment now—the Dark Ones would be through that door he could not lock, would take him as easily as one roped a larng in the spring trapping pens. Why they had not already been upon him he did not know. As he hesitated there, he heard, more as a vibration through the walls than a sound, the pounding feet. But there was no fumbling at the door. Kincar guessed that his pursuers had gone to the next level, that the closing of the door had momentarily hidden his trail. Should he—could he dodge out now and backtrack while the hunters were on the higher levels? He could not bring himself to that move. The wild slide down the well ladder in the other tower and his run through the passages had worn him down; his energy was fading fast.

What did he do now? Remain where he was until they searched from chamber to chamber and found him? He swayed to the flier, dropped on one of the seats within it, his hurt hands resting palms up on his knees.

If he had only the proper knowledge, he could be free—away without any difficulty at all. The buttons on the panel before him were frustrating—if he only knew which ones—

The vibration of the hurrying hunters reached him faintly. They were coming back down again—or could that be reinforcements arriving from below? Dully Kincar studied the controls. Nothing in his dealing with the Star men he knew had given him a hint of their machines. But he could not be taken again—he could not! Better to smash the flier and himself than to sit here tamely until they broke in.

Kincar closed his eyes, offered a wordless petition to those he served, and made a blind choice of button. Only it was the wrong one. Heat walled up about him as if a cloak had been flung about his shivering body. Heat answered that button. He counted one over, relieved that disaster had not resulted from his first choice.

A shaft of light struck upon the rounded wall before him, flashing back into his dazzled eyes. It startled him so that he triggered the third button before he thought.

He grabbed the sides of his seat in spite of the pain in his hands. His gasp was close to a scream, for the flier was shooting up, out of that well, at a speed that almost tore the air from his lungs. The machine broke out of the well, went on and on up into the sky. It must be stopped—or he would reach star space. But how to control it he had no idea.

With the faint hope that the function of the button next to the last one he had pushed might counteract it, he thrust with an urgent finger. He was right, inasmuch as that sickening rise stopped. But his flight was not halted. The flier now skimmed forward with an equally terrifying speed, as might an arrow shot from a giant bow. But for the moment Kincar was content. He was not bound for outer space, and he was headed with breath-taking speed away from the towers. He crouched on the seat, almost unable to believe his good fortune.

When he grew more accustomed to flight, he ventured to look below, keeping a good grip on the seat and fighting vertigo. The same chance that had brought his finger to the right button had also dictated the course of the flier. It was headed across the waste plain, not for the sea lowlands and the cities ruled by the Dark Ones, but toward the distant mountain range—only not so distant now—where Kincar might have a faint hope of not only surviving but eventually rejoining those at the hold.

There remained the problem of grounding the flier. Just at the moment he had no desire to experiment—until at least one mountain lay between him and pursuit. And, thinking of pursuit sent him squirming about to look behind. The Dark Ones must have more than just one such flier—would they take to the air after him? But above the rapidly diminishing dot of the fortress he could see nothing in the air.

What might have been two—three days' travel for a larng flashed below in a short space of time. Then he was above the peaks he had seen from the ship-towers, skimming—just barely skimming—over snow-crowned rock. If he only knew how to control the flier! Its speed was certainly excessive. His elation gave way once more to anxiety as he imagined what might happen should the machine crash head-on against some peak higher than its present level of flight.

16

Rescue

If no other flier arose from the ship-towers to intercept
Kincar's runaway transport, something else did. He
first knew of his danger when a piercing shriek of rage
and avid hunger carried through the rush of air dinning
at his eardrums. Compared to that challenge, Vorken's
most ambitious call was a muted whisper. Kincar
stared aloft and then shrank in the seat, for what
swooped at him now was death, a familiar death, well
known to any Gorthian who had ever roamed the
mountain ranges.

Vorken was a mord, but she was counted a pygmy
of her species. Among the frigid heights lived the giants
of her race, able to carry off a larng at their pleasure.
And their appetites were as huge as their bodies. They
could be entrapped with a triple- or quadruple-strand
net and men well versed in the tricky business to handle it, but such a netting meant days of patient waiting,
luring the creature to the ground with bait. Once on
the surface of the mountainside or plateau, they were
enough at a disadvantage to be snared, though it was
always a risky business, and no one was surprised if
such a hunting party returned minus one or more of
the hunters.

No one had ever faced a sa-mord in the air. No one

had lived through an attack made when the attacker was wing borne and free. And Kincar had no hope of surviving this one.

With the usual egotism of a man, he had reckoned that *he* was the aim of those claws, whereas, to the sa-mord he was merely an incidental part of the thing it attacked. It made its swoop from the skies, talons stretched to grasp the flier, only to discover it had not properly judged the speed of this impudent air creature, missing its strike by a foot or more.

It plunged past in an instant, screaming its furious rage, and was gone before Kincar could realize that he had not been pierced through by those claws. Had he then been able to control the flier, he might have won free or tired the creature out to the point where it would have given up the chase. But such evasive action was beyond his power. He could only stay where he was, half sheltered by the back of the seat and the windbreak, as the flier bore straight ahead, while behind, the sa-mord beat up into the sky for a second strike.

Like their smaller relatives, the sa-mords had intelligence of a sort, and most of that reasoning power was centered upon keeping its possessor not only fed but alive. The sa-mords were solitary creatures, each female having a section of hunting territory where she ruled supreme, ready to beat off any of her kind who threatened her hold on sky and earth therein. And to such battles each brought accumulated knowledge of feint, attack, and the proper use of her own strength.

So when the sa-mord now struck for the second time, from a yet higher point, she had recalculated the speed of the flier and came down in a dive that should have brought her a little ahead and facing the enemy with waiting claws, a favorite fighting position.

Only again mechanical speed proved her undoing,

for she hit directly on the flier's nose. The windbreak was driven into her softer underparts by the force of that meeting. Claws raked across the shield, catching on the seats, as she squalled at her hurt. Kincar, wedged in as flat as he could get, felt rather than saw that gaping beak that snapped just an inch or two above him as blood spurted from torn arteries to flow greasily.

The machine faltered, dipped, fought against that struggling weight impaled on its nose. It was losing altitude as the sa-mord beat and tore at it. Only the fact that the flier was metal, and so impervious to her attack, saved Kincar during those few moments before they were carried into a thicket of snow-line scrub trees. There the sa-mord's body acted as a shock absorber and cushion as they slammed to a final stop.

Kincar, the breath beaten out of him by the sharp impact, lay where he was, the stench of the torn creature thick in the air. Gone was the heat that had enfolded him. Shivering in the lash of mountain wind, he at last fought his way out of the grisly wreckage and staggered along the splintered swath the flier had cut. One sa-mord to a hunting territory was the custom. But there were lesser things that could scent blood and raw meat from afar. Weaponless he could not face up to such carrion eaters. So, guided more by instinct than plan, he reeled downslope.

Luckily the flier had not crashed on one of the higher crests, and the incline was not so straight that he could not pick a path. Here the scrub wood was thin. It was possible to set landmarks ahead to keep that path from circling.

It must be far past midday, and he would have to find shelter. From upslope there came a muffled yapping, then a growling, rising to roaring defiance. The scavengers had found their feast, and there was no hope of returning to the wreckage. In fact, that din spurred Kincar to a faster pace, until he lost his footing and fell forward, to roll into a snowdrift.

Gasping, spitting snow, he struggled up, knowing that to lie there was to court death. Only by keeping on his feet and moving did he have the thinnest chance. Fortunately the sky was clear of clouds; no storm threatened.

That fall and slide had brought him into a valley with a trickle of stream at its bottom. The water was dark, flowing quickly, with no skim of ice. He wavered down to it and went on his knees. Now he could feel the faint, very faint warmth exuding from the riverlet. This must be one of the hot streams, such as he had discovered in the hold valley. He had only to trace it back to its source and that heat would grow, promising him some protection against the cold of the coming night.

It was an effort to get to his feet again, to flog his bruised body along. But somehow he kept moving, aware through the fog of exhaustion that there were now trails of steam above the water, that the temperature in the valley was rising. Choking and coughing from the fumes, he fell against a boulder and clung there. He had to have the heat, but could he stand the lung-searing exhalations of the water?

Slowly he went down beside the rock, certain he could go no farther, and no longer wanting to try. It all assumed the guise of a dream, and the inertia of one caught in a nightmare weighted him. There was the grit of stone against his cheek and then nothing at all.

The sa-mord loomed above him. He had been very wrong. It was not killed by the flier, and now it had tracked him down. In a moment he would be rent by claw and beak. Only it was carrying him up—higher than the mountains! They were swinging out over the waste to the ship-towers. A flier bore him—no sa-mord but a flier! The machine was rising at the nose—it would turn over, spill him down—

"Get him up if you have to lash him! We can take no chances on this climb—"

Words coming out of the air, words without meaning. Warm—it was warm again. He had not been killed in that fall from the flier. Now he was lapped in the waters of the hot riverlet, being borne with its current. Watery, he saw the world only through a mist of water, and before him bobbed another dim figure. Then that shadowy shape turned, and he saw its face and knew that there was no escape. Lord Dillan! They had traced him, and he was once more a prisoner.

"Not so!" He heard his own cry as shrill as a mord's scream as he tried vainly to win free of the current, away from the Dark One. But it was no use; he could not move and the riverlet carried him on.

It was night, but not the total dark of the U-Sippar dungeon, for stars swung across Lor's Shield resting above him. And those stars moved—or did he? Dreamily he tried to work out that problem. The homely smell of larng sweat had driven away the stink of the river. But he was still swinging as if cradled in water.

"There is the beacon! We are almost in now—"

In where? U-Sippar? The ship-tower fortress? He had solved the mystery of the movement around, under, about him, realizing that he was lashed securely in a hunter's net swung between two of the burden larngs. But how much was real and how much was a dream he could not tell. He closed heavy eyelids, worn to a state of fatigue in which nothing at all mattered.

But perhaps he was too tired for sleep, for he was aware of arriving in a courtyard, and roused again to see the one who loosed the fastenings of his net.

It had been no use, that wild attempt at escape, for it was Lord Dillan who gathered him up and carried him into light, warmth, and sound. They were back at the ship-towers, and now would come the questioning—

They must have returned him to the padded chamber. He was lying on the softness of the bench there. Feeling it, he kept his eyes closed obstinately. Let them think he was unconscious.

"Kincar—"

He tensed.

"Kincar—"

There was no mistaking that voice. They might duplicate Lord Dillan but—the Lady Asgar? He opened his eyes. She was half-smiling, though watching him with a healer's study. And she was bundled in cold-season riding clothes, her hair fastened up tightly beneath a fur hood. Vorken sat on her shoulder appearing to examine Kincar with a measure of the same searching scrutiny.

"This is the hold?" He doubted the evidence of his eyes; he had been so sure he was elsewhere.

"This is the hold. And you are safe, thanks be to Vorken. Is that not true, my strong-winged one?"

Vorken bent her head to rub her crest of bone peak caressingly against the Lady's chin.

"We were hunting in the peaks and she came to us, leading us to a feast—" Asgar's expression was one of faint distaste. "And from there it was easy to trace your path, Kincar. Now"—she stooped over him with a horn cup in her hand while someone behind raised his head and shoulders so that he might drink—"get this inside of you that you may tell us your story, for we have a fear that time grows very late indeed."

It was Lord Dillan who supported him. But his own Lord Dillan and not the dark master of the ship-towers. Braced comfortably against that strong shoulder, Kincar told his story, tersely with none of a song-smith's embroidery of word. Only one thing he could not describe plainly, and that was what had happened to him in the ruined shrine. And that they did not ask of him. When he told of his meeting with the fugitives at the shore, Lord Dillan spoke for the first time.

"This we have heard in part. Murren could not master Cim, and the beast took his own path. He brought them to our gates, and they were found by Kapal and a foraging party. We have heard their story, and it is a black one." There was a dark shadow of pain in his eyes. "It will be for your hearing later. So—you were taken by the ruler's men," he prompted, and Kincar continued.

There was Vorken's providential appearance on the field where he had been condemned to death, and then the interference of the Dark Lord Dillan—

The man who held him tensed at his description. "Not only Rud—but *I*—here too?"

"Did we not know that it would be so for some of us?" queried the Lady Asgar. "And in the end that may prove the one weapon we have. But where did they then take you, Kincar?"

His memories of the ship-towers were so deeply etched that his account of the action there was more vivid. Both of the Star-born were moved by his recounting of his trial by fear.

"A conditioner!" Lord Dillan spat the word. "To have perverted that!"

"But that is a small perversion among so many," Asgar pointed out, "for their whole life here is a perversion, as well we know. Because that particular machine is a tool known to you, Dillan, it may strike more deeply home, but it is in my mind that they have made use of all their knowledge—our knowledge—to weld slave chains. And mark this—the conditioner was defeated by something native to this Gorth! Kincar believes that he was sent on this path, and it seems to me that he is right, very right! But you escaped from these earth-bound ships, and how was that done?" she demanded of the young man.

In retelling, his flight from the weird fortress sounded matter-of-fact and without difficulty, though Kincar strongly doubted that he could face it again. Action was far easier to take in sudden improvisation than when one knew what lay in wait ahead.

When he had done, the drink they had given him began its work. The aches of his bruised body faded into a lethargy, and he slipped into a deep sleep.

He woke again suddenly, without any of the normal lazy translation from drowsiness to full command. And when he opened his eyes, it was to see the youth from the seashore hut seated not far away, his chin cupped in both hands, studying Kincar as if the other held some answer to a disturbing puzzle. The very force of that gaze, thought Kincar, was enough to draw one out of sleep. And he asked, "What do you want?"

The other smiled oddly. "To see you, Kincar s'Rud."

"Which you are doing without hindrance. But there is more than just looking upon me that you wish—"

The boy shrugged. "Perhaps. Though your very existence is a marvel in this world. Kincar s'Rud," he repeated the name gravely, not as if he were addressing its owner, but more as one might utter some incantation. "Kincar s'Rud—Kathal s'Rud—"

Kincar sat up on the pad couch. He was stiff and sore, but he was alert and no longer weary to his very bones.

"Kincar s'Rud I know well," he observed. "But who is Kathal s'Rud?"

The other laughed. "Look at him! They have told me many things, these strange lords here, and few of them are believable, save to one who will swallow a song-smith's tales open-brained. But almost I can trust in every word when I look upon you. It seems, though we can both claim a Lord Rud for a sire, it is not the same Lord Rud. And that smacks of truth, for you and I are not alike."

"Lord Rud's son—" For a second Kincar was befuddled. Lord Dillan had spoken of brothers—no, half brothers—who could name him kin. But they had gone with the Star ships. Then he understood. Not his father—but the Lord Rud of this Gorth, that man softened by good living, rotted with his absolute power, whom he had fronted in U-Sippar. "But I thought—"

"That there were no half-bloods here? Aye!" The boy was all one bitter protest. "They have even spread it about that such births are impossible, like the offspring of a mord and a suard. But it is true, though mostly we are slain at birth—if our fathers know of it. To live always under a death sentence, enforced not only by the Dark Ones, but by your other kin as well—it is not easy."

"Lord Rud found out about you; that was why you were running?"

"Aye. Murren, who was guardsman to my mother's kin, saved me twice. But he was handled as you saw for his trouble. Better he himself had knocked me on the head! I am a nothing thing, being neither truly of one blood or the other."

As he had studied Kincar, so now the other reversed the process. This was no duplicate other self, no physical twin, as were the two Dillans. So some other laws of chance and change had intervened between them. Kathal, he judged, was the younger by several birth seasons, and he had the fine-drawn, worn face, the tense, never-relaxed body of one who, as he had just pointed out, lived ever with danger. No happy memories of a Wurd or of the satisfying life of Styr were behind him. Would *he* have been as Kathal had he been born into this Gorth?

"You are safe now." Kincar tried to reassure him.

Kathal simply stared at him as one looks at a child who does not understand how foolishly he speaks.

"Am I? There is no safety ever for one who is s'Rud—no matter how it may be in the world from which *you* came."

"The Lords will change that—"

Again that bitter laugh. "Aye, your Lords amaze me. I am told that all here are full or half-blood—save for the refugees and freed slaves you have drawn in. But what weapons have your lords? How can they stand up against the might of all Gorth? For all Gorth will be marshaled against this hold when the truth is known. Best build another of these 'gates' of which they speak and charge through it before you feel Rud's fingers on your throat!"

And Kincar, remembering the ship-towers, the flier, could agree that other weapons and wonders must rest in the hands of the Dark Ones. His confidence was shaken for a moment.

"—and a deft server you shall find me!" That half sentence heralded Lord Dillan, who pushed through the door curtain, walking with exaggerated care because he held in both of his hands an eating bowl, lacy with steam and giving off an aroma that immediately impressed upon Kincar how long it had been since he had eaten. Lord Bardon was close behind him, his fingers striving to keep in one bundle several drinking horns of different sizes. Following on his heels came the remainder of the Star Lords, dwarfing the younger half-Gorthians with their bulk.

Kathal slipped from his seat and backed against the wall. He gave the appearance of a man about to make

196

a lost stand against impossible odds. It was Lord Jon who put down the leather bottle he was carrying and smiled.

"Both in one netting. Feed yours, Dillan, and I'll settle this one and see that his tongue is properly moistened for speech." His clasp on Kathal's shoulder was the light one he would have used on his own son, and though the half-Gorthian fugitive had not lost his suspicion, he did not try to elude that grip.

Kincar spooned up the solid portion of the stew and drank the rich gravy. He had had no such meal since he had ridden out of Styr. Journeycake and dried meat were good enough for travelers, but they held no flavor.

"This," announced Lord Bardon, but his tone was light enough to war with the sense of his words, "is a council of war. We have come to learn all you can tell us, sons of Rud."

Perhaps Kathal flinched at a title that in this world meant shame and horror. But Kincar found it natural and was pleased at that link with the soft-spoken but sword-wary men about him. A measure of that confidence that had been frayed by Kathal's suspicions was restored. He had seen the Dark Ones, and to his mind none of them were matches for the Star men that he knew.

"We shall begin"—Lord Dillan took charge of the assembly as he was wont to do—"with a naming of names. Tell us, Kathal, who are the Dark Ones—give us a full roll call of their number."

17

"It can never be set one piece within the other properly again!"

Kincar sat back on his heels. There was a broad smear of suard fat across his cheek where his hand had brushed unnoticed, and before him lay a puzzle of bits of metal salvaged from the broken flier. Brought from the point where it had cracked up, the machine was in the process of being reassembled by the Star Lords and half-bloods alike, neither certain of the ultimate results.

Lord Dillan sighed. "Almost it would seem so," he conceded. "I am a technician of sorts, but as a mechanic it appears I have a great many limitations. If I could only remember more!" He ran *his* greasy hands through his close-cropped dark-red hair. "Let this be a lesson to you, boy. Take notice of what you see in your youth— it may be required of you to duplicate it later. I have flown one of these—but to rebuild it is another matter."

Lord Jon, who had been lying belly-down on the courtyard pavement to inspect parts of the frame they had managed so far to fit together, smiled.

"All theory and no practice, Dillan? What we need is a tape record to guide us—"

"Might as well wish for a new flier complete, Lord."

Vulth got to his feet and stretched to relieve cramped muscles. "Give me a good sword tail, and I'll open that box for you without this need for patching broken wire and shafts together."

Lord Bardon, who had earlier withdrawn from their efforts to fit the unfitable together, protesting that he had never possessed any talent for machine assembly, laughed.

"And where do we recruit a tail for spear-festing, Vulth? Lay a summoning on the mountain trees to turn them into warriors for your ordering? From all accounts any assault straight into the face of danger will not work this time. I wonder—" He was studying the parts laid out on the stones. "That gear to the left of your foot, Dillan—it seems close in size to the rod Jon just bolted in. Only a suggestion, of course."

Lord Dillan picked up the piece and held it to the rod. Then he observed solemnly, "Any more suggestions, Bard? It is plain that *you* are the mechanic here."

Kincar was excited. "Look, Lord. If that fits there, then does not this and this go so?" He slipped the parts into the pattern he envisioned. He might not know Star magic, but these went together with a rightness his eyes approved.

Dillan threw up his hands in a gesture of mock defeat. "It would seem that the totally unschooled are better at this employment. Perhaps a little knowledge is a deterrent rather than a help. Go ahead, children, and see what you can do without my hindrance."

In the end, with all of them assisting, they had the flier rebuilt.

"The question remains," Lord Bardon said, "will it now fly?"

"There is only one way to test that." Before any of them could protest, Lord Dillan was in the seat behind the controls. However, even as his hand moved toward

200

the row of buttons, Kincar was beside him, knowing that he could not let the other make that trial alone.

Perhaps Dillan would have ordered him out, but it was too late for that, as inadvertently the Star Lord had pushed the right button and they were rising—not with the terrifying speed Kincar had known in his last flier trip, but slowly, with small complaints and buzzes from the engine.

"At least," Lord Dillan remarked, "she did not blow up at once. But I would not care to race her—"

They were above the hold towers now. And Vorken, seeing them rise past her chosen roost, took to the air in company, flying in circles about the machine and uttering cries of astonishment and dismay. Men walking, men riding larngs she understood and had been accustomed to from fledglinghood. But men in her own element were different and worrying.

Kincar, with only too vivid memories of the mountain sa-mord, tried to wave her away. Vorken could not smash the flier with her weight as had the giant of her species. But if she chose to fly into Lord Dillan's face, she might well bring them to grief. Her circles grew closer, as she swung in behind the windbreak, her curiosity getting the better of her caution. Then she made a landing on the back of the seats and squatted, her long neck outstretched between the two who sat there, interested in what they would do next.

"Do you approve?" Lord Dillan asked her.

She squawked in an absent-minded fashion, as if to brush aside foolish questions. And seeing that she was minded to be quiet, Kincar did not try to dislodge her.

Dillan began to try out the repaired craft. It did not respond too quickly to the controls governing change of altitude or direction. But it did handle, and he thought it could be safely used for the purpose they planned. After flying down the wide valley guarded by the hold and making a circle about the mountain walls, he brought the machine back for a bumpy but safe landing in the courtyard.

"She is no AA job, but she will take us there—" was his verdict given to the hold party and the natives from four liberated slave gangs. The hold archers now kept a regular watch on the mountain road and freed all unfortunates dragged through that territory.

Kapal had assumed command of these men, and out of those who still possessed some stamina and spirit, he was hammering a fighting tail of which he often despaired but bullied and drilled all the more grimly because they fell so far below his hopes. He had taken readily, greedily, to the use of the bows and was employing both the men and the few women from the exslave gangs to manufacture more. Now he insisted that it was time for him to lead his band in some foray on their own.

"It is this way, Lord," he had sought out Bardon the night before to urge. "They have been slaves too long. They think like slaves, believing that no man can stand up to the Dark Ones. But let us once make even a party of slave-driving Hands surrender, or rather let us blood our arrows well on such eaters of dirt, and they will take new heart. They must have a victory before they can think themselves once more men!"

"If we had time, then I would say aye to that, Kapal, for your reasoning is that of a leader who knows well the ways of fighting men. But time we do not have. Let the Dark Ones discover us, and they have that which will blot us out before finger can meet upon finger in a closing fist. Nay, our move must be fast, sure, and merciless. And it should come very soon!"

Kathal had given them the key to what might be their single advantage. Occasionally the Dark Ones assembled at the ship-tower fortress. In spite of their covert internecine warfare, their jealousies and private feuds, they still kept to some fellowship and a certain amount of exchange of supplies, news and man power.

Though they laughed at native traditions, stamping out any whenever they found them, they themselves were not wholly free of the desire for symbolic celebrations. And one such, perhaps the most rigidly kept, was that marking their first landing on Gorth. For this anniversary they assembled from all over the planet, making a two-day festival of the gathering. It seldom ended without some bloodshed, though dueling was frowned upon. The natives, excluded from the meeting, forbidden even to approach within a day's journey of the ship-towers, knew that often a Lord did not return from the in-gathering and that his domain was appropriated by another.

"It has been our hope that they would continue to deal with each other so," Kathal had said, "using their might against their own kind. But always it works to our ill, for those Dark Ones who treated us with some measure of forbearing were always the ones to return not, and the more ruthless took their lands. Of late years there have been fewer disappearances—"

"How many Lords are there left?" Lord Frans had wanted to know.

Kathal spread his fingers as if to use them in telling off numbers. "Who can truthfully say, Lord? There are fifty domains, each with an overlord. Of these perhaps a third have sons, younger brothers, kinsmen. Of their females we know little. They live secretly under heavy guard. So secret do they keep them that there are now rumors they are very, very few. So few that the Lords—" He had paused, a dark flush staining his too-thin face.

"So few," Lord Dillan had taken that up, "that now

such as your Lord Rud has a forbidden household, and perhaps others do likewise. Yet they will not allow their half-blood children to live."

Kathal shook his head. "If the Lords break that law, Lord, then they are held up to great shame among their kindred. To them we are as beasts, things of no account. Mayhap here and there a half-blood, who was secretly born, lives for a space of years. But mostly they are slain young. Only because my mother had a sister who kept her close did I come to man's age."

"Say perhaps one hundred?" Lord Bardon had kept on reckoning the opposition.

"Half again more," Kathal replied.

"And they will all be at the ship-towers twelve days from now?"

"Aye, Lord, that is the time of the in-gathering."

The hold began their own preparations, working all day and far into the night, for if at no other time all the Dark Ones would be together, then they must strike here and now. They dared not wait another whole year, and they could never hope to campaign against fortresses beaded clear across Gorth.

As soon as they were certain the flier could take to the air again, the first party, mounted on the pick of the larngs moved out, armed and prepared for a long ride across the mountain trails that the inner men had shown them.

Kapal and his ragged crew, or the best of them, padded through the secret ways of the mountain with Ospik for a guide, heading for the agreed-upon point overlooking the waste plain on which the ship-towers stood.

Kincar had expected to ride with the other half-bloods in the mounted party. But, as the only one who had ever been at the ships, he was delegated to join the Star Lords.

The flier would carry four at a time—reluctantly—but it *would* rise and, at a speed greater than a larng's extended gallop, get them over the ranges to the last tall peak from which they could look down upon their goal. All wore the silver clothing insulated against the chill, giving them more freedom of movement than the scale coats and leather garments the Gorthians and half-Gorthians were used to. And Kincar, clad in a suit hastily cut to his size, moved among them looking like a boy among his elders.

On the heights they took cover, but four pairs of far-seeing glasses passed from hand to hand, Kincar having them in his turn. And so they witnessed the arrival of swarms of fliers at the towers.

"That makes one hundred and ten," Lord Bardon reported. "But each carries several passengers."

Lord Dillan had the glasses at the moment.

"I wonder, Bard—?"

"Wonder what?"

"Whether those ships were ever deactivated?"

"They must have been! Surely they wouldn't have built them into those walls otherwise—"

"Ours were not. In fact, Rotherberg said that he didn't believe they could be."

"Do you mean," Kincar demanded, "that they could take off in those ships right now, as the Star Lords did in our Gorth?"

"It would solve a lot of our problems if they would do just that, but I hardly think they will oblige us by trying it."

Lord Dillan did not answer that. He continued to hold the glasses to his eyes as if memorizing every detail of the ships.

"No arrivals for a long time now," remarked Lord Bardon. "Do you suppose they are all here?"

"It would appear so. We'll wait until morning to be

sure." Lord Dillan was still on watch. "We'll camp and leave a scout to keep an eye on them."

The camp was a temporary affair, set up in a gulch, with a heat box to provide them with the equivalent of a fire and journey rations to eat. Kincar took his turn at scout duty close to dawn. There had been no more arrivals at the ship-towers in the darkness, and the party from the hold concluded that all the Dark Ones must be in the fortress.

"We could use double our numbers," Lord Bardon remarked as they broke their fast.

"I could wish more for Rotherberg of Lacee."

"Hmm." Lord Bardon gazed hard at Lord Dillan. "Still thinking of that, are you? But none of us are engineers—we would not stand here if we were. Those who had that in their blood chose to go with the ships."

"Nevertheless, I believe we should keep the idea in mind!"

"Oh, that we shall do." Lord Bardon laughed. "Should I chance upon the proper controls, I shall set them for a takeoff. Meanwhile, the escape hatches seem the best entrances—we should be able to reach them from the tops of those walls. Shall we head for the nearest?"

"We shall. And before it grows too light."

Again the flier was pressed into ferry service, transporting their small band across the waste to the base of one of the corridor walls close to the foot of the nearest ship-tower. Lord Sim swung overhead a rope with a hook attached—twin to the weapon Murren had used. The prongs caught on the top of the wall and held against his heaviest tugs, and by the rope they climbed up.

Lord Tomm planted himself with his back against the smooth side of the ancient ship, bracing his feet a little apart to take weight, and the lighter Lord Jon stood on his shoulders, facing inward so that he could touch an oval outline that showed faintly on the ship. With a tool from his belt he traced that outline carefully, and then pushed. It took two such tracings to cut through the sealing, but at last the door came free and they were in the ship.

Kincar was the third inside, sniffing again that odd musty odor of the silent tower. But Lord Frans, following him, gave an exclamation of surprise as he stood in the corridor.

"This is the *Morris!*"

"Their Morris," corrected Lord Dillan. "You can guide us, Frans. This is twin to your father's ship—"

"The control chamber—" Lord Frans frowned at the wall. "It has been so many years. Aye, we'll want that first!"

"Why?" Lord Jon wanted to know. He was looking about him with some of Kincar's curiosity. Himself two generations younger than the original space travelers, the ships were almost as strange to him as they were to the half-Gorthian.

"If she is still activated, we will be able to use the scanner."

While that meant nothing to Kincar, it apparently did to the others.

Lord Frans guided them, not to a center well ladder-stair such as Kincar and his captors had used, but to a narrower and more private way, hardly large enough for the Star men to negotiate. The steps were merely loops of metal on which to rest toes and fingers. They went up and up until Lord Frans disappeared through a well opening and Lord Bardon after him. Then Kincar climbed into one of the most bewildering rooms he had ever seen.

There were four padded, cushioned objects, which were a cross between a seat and a bunk. Each was swung on a complicated base of springs and yielding supports before banks of levers and buttons to which the controls of the small flier were the playthings of a child. Above each of these boards was a wide oblong of opaque stuff, mirrors that reflected nothing in the room. Kincar remained where he was, a little overawed by this array of Star magic, with a feeling that to press the wrong button here might send them all off into space.

Lord Dillan walked across the chamber. "Astrogator." He dropped his hand on the back of one of those odd seats, and it trembled under the slight pressure. "Pilot," he indicated another. "Astro-Pilot." That was the third. "Com-Tech." The fourth and last was the seat Lord Dillan chose to sit in.

As soon as his weight settled in the chair-bed, the bank of buttons slid noiselessly forward so it was well within his reach. He was in no hurry to put it to use, deliberating over his choice before he pressed a button. Above the control bank that square mirror flashed rippling bars of yellow light, and Lord Jon broke out eagerly, "She is still alive?"

"At least the coms are in." Again the words meant nothing to Kincar. But he would have paid little attention to any speech at the moment. He was too intrigued by what was happening on the screen. It was as if Lord Dillan had opened a window. Spread out there was a wide picture of the wastelands and the mountain range as they existed outside the ship.

He had only an instant to make identification before that picture changed, and they were looking at a room crowded with a mass of metal parts and machines he could not have set name to—

"Engine room," breathed Lord Jon softly, wonderingly.

Another movement of Lord Dillan's finger, and they

had a new view—a place of tanks, empty, dusty, long disused.

"Hydro—"

So they inspected the vitals of the ship, cabin to cabin. But in all their viewing nothing was living, nor was there any indication that anyone had been there for a very long time. At last Lord Dillan leaned back, sending his support jiggling.

"She is not the one—"

Lord Bardon was studying the banks of controls fronting the pilot's seat. "They would be more likely to hole up in the *Gangee*. After all she was the flag ship. Hm—" He did not sit down in the pilot's place but leaned across to move a lever. There was a brilliant flash of red in a small bulb there, and from somewhere about them a voice rasped in the speech of the Star ways.

"She's still hot!" Lord Jon exploded.

Lord Dillan smiled, a chill smile that Kincar knew he would not care to have turned in his direction.

"And she will be hotter." He arose and crossed to join Lord Bardon. "Five hours ought to give us time enough. Let us see now—" He counted levers and studs, peered closely at dials, and then his hands flew, weaving a pattern over the board. "Let us be on the way now. We'll try the *Gangee* next."

"She'll lift?" demanded Lord Tomm.

"She'll certainly try. In any event she'll wreck this part of the building."

They made their way back to the wall top, out into the early morning sunshine. Lord Dillan pivoted, examining each of the other towers.

"Might as well split up now. Jon, you and Rodric, Sim and Tomm, get in those other end ships. If they are empty, set them to blow—five hours from now or thereabouts. Bring with you any of"—he rattled off a

209

string of queer words incomprehensible to Kincar—"you come across in their store rooms. We'll try for the *Gangee*."

They nodded and separated, heading for different ships.

18

Once More a Gate—

There was a different "feel" to the *Gangee*. They made their entrance through the old escape port of the ship without opposition or discovery. But, as they clustered together at the foot of the ladder to the control cabin, even Kincar was conscious of a faint heat radiating from the walls about them, a lack of dead air long sealed in.

"This is the one." Lord Bardon was satisfied.

"Controls again?" Lord Frans wanted to know.

"Just so!" The words were bitten off as if Lord Dillan was reluctant to make that climb. Did he think they might find others occupying that chamber?

But he sped up the ladder, Lord Bardon at his heels, and the rest strung out behind. They climbed by closed doors on every level. And twice Kincar, brushing against the inner fabric with his shoulder, felt a vibration through the ship, like a beat of motive power.

The control cabin, when they reached it, was, at first inspection, very little different from that of the *Morris*—the same four chairs, the same banks of controls, the same vision plates above them. Once more Lord Dillan seated himself in the Com-Tech's place and pressed a stud. They glimpsed the outside world, and then the picture changed. The engine room—but this one was not silent, dust-shrouded. Rods moved on dials set in casing. The Hydro garden was stretches of green stuff growing, and the Star Lords were surprised.

"Do you think they are planning a take-off?" asked Lord Jon.

"More likely they keep the *Gangee* in blast condition as a symbol," Lord Dillan replied. "Which may be their salvation now—"

Once more the picture flickered and cleared. Kincar started. It was so vivid, so clear, that he had the sensation of looking through an open window into a crowded room, for it was crowded.

An exclamation in his own tongue burst from Lord Frans, echoed by one from Lord Jon. It was an assemblage of the Dark Ones they spied upon.

"You—Great Spirit of Space! Dillan, there you are!" Lord Bardon's voice shook as he identified one of those men. "And Rud—that is truly Rud! Lacee—Mac—Bart—but Bart's dead! He died of the spinning fever years ago. And—and—" His face was a gray-white now beneath its weathered brown, his eyes wide, stricken. "Alis—Dillan, it's Alis!" He flung away toward the other door of the chamber.

Lord Dillan barked an order, sharp enough to send Kincar moving. The other Star Lords were frozen, hypnotized by what they saw. Only to Kincar to whom it was just a company of aliens did that command have meaning.

"Stop him! Don't let him leave this cabin!"

Lord Bardon was a third again his size, and Kincar did not know how he could obey, but there was no mistaking the frantic urgency of the order. He hurled himself across the door, clasping the stay rods on either side imposing his body between Lord Bardon and the portal. Lord Dillan was hurrying to them, but he did

212

not reach there before his fellow had crashed into Kincar, slamming the half-Gorthian back painfully against the ship metal, before he began tearing at him, trying to drag him away.

A hand caught at Lord Bardon, brought him partly around, and then a palm struck first one cheek and then the other in a head-rocking duo of slaps.

"Bardon!"

Lord Bardon staggered, that strained stare in his eyes beginning to break. Lord Dillan spoke swiftly in their own language until Lord Bardon gave a broken little cry and covered his face with both hands. Then Lord Dillan turned to the others.

"They are not there, understand?" He spoke with a slow and heavy emphasis, designed to drive every word not only into their ears, but also into their minds. "Those down there are not the ones we know—knew. I am not that Dillan, nor is he me."

Lord Jon caught a quivering underlip between his teeth. He was still watching the screen longingly, and Lord Dillan spoke directly to him.

"That is not your father you see there, Jon. Keep that in mind! This I know." He swung upon them all. "We must have no speech with these, for our sakes—perhaps for theirs. There is only one thing to do. They have poisoned this Gorth, as we to a lesser extent poisoned ours. And now they must go forth from it—"

He had laid his hand on the back of the pilot's seat when Bardon spoke hoarsely.

"You can't blast them off without any warning!"

"We will not. But they shall only have enough to ensure their lives during take-off. There must be payment for what has been done here—the risk they shall run in entering exile will be toward the settlement of that account."

The Star Lords were occupied with their problem, but Kincar had been watching the screen again. Now he ventured to interrupt.

"Lord, are they able to see us, as we do them?"

Dillan whirled, his head up, to front the vision plate. There could be no mistake; the party they spied upon were quiet, all heads turned to face the screen. And the blank astonishment of most of their expressions was altering to concern. That other Lord Dillan moved, advancing toward them, until his head alone covered three-quarters of the plate.

It was something out of a troubled dream to see one Dillan stare at the other, if only from a screen. A huge hand moved across the corner of the plate and was gone again. Then a voice boomed out above them, speaking the Star tongue. Dillan, *their* Dillan, snapped a small switch beneath the plate and made answer. Then his hand swept down breaking contact, both eye and voice.

"We have little time," he said unhurriedly. "Dog that door so that they may not enter until they burn through—"

It was Lord Frans and Lord Jon who obeyed. Lord Bardon remained by the pilot's chair—until Dillan turned on him.

"We shall give them more than just a slim chance, Bard. Once in space they can make a fresh start. We are not dooming them—"

"I know— I know! But *will* the ship lift? Or will it—" His voice faded to a half whisper.

"Now," Dillan told them all, "get out—away from here—as fast as you can move!"

Kincar was on the ladder. The fear of being trapped and torn skyward was very real. Lord Jon and Lord Frans came after him. All three were in the outer air before Lord Bardon joined them. And he lingered in the hatch, one hand on the rope, waiting.

They were hailed by the other parties. Lord Jon waved them off with wild arm signals. Then Lord Bardon dropped from the hatch and a last silver figure appeared in the oval opening. He brought that door to behind him and slid down the rope.

"Run, you fools!" he shouted, and Kincar found himself pounding away from the *Gangee* along the top of the wall. He had no idea how a space ship, especially one built up by masonry would take off, but he could guess that the results would be earthshaking at ground level.

A large arm clamped a viselike grip about his waist, and Lord Dillan gasped, "Jump now, son!"

He was borne along by the other from the top of the wall. They hit hard and rolled. Then he was punched into a ball half under the other's bulk as the ground under them rocked and broke. There was the clamor of mistreated metal, the rumble of a world coming to an end, and a flash so brilliant that it blinded him—to be followed by a clap of noise and a silence so complete that it was as if all sound had been reft away.

Broken lumps of stone rained noiselessly from the sky. There was no sound at all. Kincar struggled free of a hold that was now only a limp weight. He sat up shakily, his head ringing, red and orange jags of light darting back and forth before his eyes when he tried to focus on his surroundings. His groping hands were on warm flesh, and then on stickiness that clung to his fingers. He rubbed impatiently at his eyes, trying to clear them. But, above all else, the dead silence was frightening.

He could see now, if only dimly. Red crawled sluggishly over a silver back beside his knee. Dazed, he rubbed his eyes again. A ringing began in his ears, worse when he moved, making it very hard to think—

But he could move. Kincar bent over the quiet body

beside him. There was a gash on the shoulder, a tear in both the silver clothing and the flesh beneath it. Already the bleeding was growing less. Cautiously he tried to move the other, exposing Lord Dillan's face slack and pale. The Star Lord was still breathing. Kincar steadied the heavy head on his arm and ripped open the sealing of the tunic. Under his fingers there was a steady heart beat, though it seemed too slow. The flier—if he could find the flier and the supplies on it—

Kincar settled Dillan's head back on the ground and stumbled to his feet. He had an odd sensation that if he moved too suddenly he might fly apart.

Before he could turn away, another silver figure hunched up from the ground. He could see Lord Jon's mouth open and shut in a grimed face, but he could not hear a word the other said. Then others ran toward them. Miraculously they had all survived the blast-off of the *Gangee,* though for long, anxious moments they were afraid that Bardon had been lost. He was discovered at last, stunned, but still alive, on the other side of a cracked and riven wall.

Kincar was deafened, unable to understand the others as they gathered at the flier. Dillan, revived, bandaged, and propped up against a heap of rubble, was giving orders. Both Jon and Bardon were unable to walk without support, and the rest were busy exploring the remaining ships and coming back to report to Dillan. Twice they brought boxes to be piled at the improvised camp site.

Lord Frans used the flier to ferry their spoil and the injured to a point well out in the waste, several miles from the ship-towers. Where the *Gangee* had formed the core of the queer structure, there was now a vast crater, avoided by the Star men, smoking in the morning air. And the walls that had tied it to its sister ships were riven, reduced to gravel-rubble in places. Study-

216

ing the remains, Kincar marveled that any one of them had survived. He might have been even more deeply impressed by their good fortune had he possessed the information shared by the men around him.

"—took off to the mountains—"

He had been watching soundlessly moving lips so long, with a growing frustration, that at first he did not realize he had caught those words, faint as a whisper, through the din in his head. Lord Frans was making a report of some importance, judging by the demeanor of those about him.

Men scattered to the ships at a trot, and the flier returned. Lord Dillan and Kincar were motioned aboard her, to be transported to the mid-point camp. Then the others came in groups until they were all well away from the ship-towers. They must have triggered the other ships, all of them. Those slim silver towers would follow the *Gangee* out into space, untenanted and derelict.

Again his ears cleared, and he caught a sharp hail. A string of mounted men were riding out in the waste, the party from the hold. They rode at a full gallop, as men might go into battle, and Vulth spurred well ahead, a Vulth shouting news as he came. He threw himself from his mount and ran up, to skid to a stop before Lord Dillan, his aspect wild.

"That demon—the one with your form, Lord—he has turned the freed slaves against us!"

Kincar noted an empty saddle among the oncoming party. Where was Jonathal? Two of the other men were wounded.

"They will circle back to the hold—"

Lord Dillan cut through that crisply. "Aye, that is his wisest move. So we must get there speedily. Frans, you take the controls—Sim—"

"Not you, Dillan!" That was Lord Bardon's protest.

"Most certainly me! Who else can face him so successfully and reveal him to be what he is? And"—his eyes went to Kincar—"and you, Kincar. This may be the time, guardian, for you to use that power—"

Dillan's energy got them on the flier after a flood of orders had sent the mounted party around to come at the hold from the plains side with the remainder of the Star Lords in their company, leaving the wounded, Lord Bardon and Lord Jon to stay at the waste camp and check on the blast-off of the rest of the ships.

The flier lifted over the ridge, heading straight for the hold. Lord Frans pushed the limping motor to its utmost, and there was no talk among the men in her. A familiar peak cut the sky before them—they were almost to the valley.

"He'll use your face as his passport," Lord Sim commented.

"Asgar will know the truth."

Aye, the Lady Asgar would be able to tell true from false, but could she distinguish that in time? And how had the false Lord Dillan managed to get out of the *Gangee* before she blasted into space? Kincar speculated concerning that, but, having seen the preoccupation of his companions, thought it better not to ask for any explanations.

From the air the hold appeared to be as it always had been—until one marked a body lying before the door of the main hall in the courtyard. Save for that grim sight there was no other sign of life—or death.

Frans brought the flier down in the courtyard. Now the ringing in Kincar's ears could not blot out the clamor issuing from the hall. He was on his feet, his sword in hand, but he had not moved faster than Lord Dillan. And running side by side they entered the core of the hold.

A handful of Gorthians, a women among them, were

218

backed against the far wall—but they were aimed and waiting. Towering among them stood the Lady Asgar. And she faced a silver figure who was the duplicate of the man beside Kincar. Fan-wise behind the false lord was a rabble of ex-slaves. Kapal, writhing feebly as if he would still be on his feet to match blades, lay with the Lady Asgar's people. And beside her, half-crouched to spring at the false Dillan's throat, was Kathal s'Rud.

The hold people were at bay, held so by the weapon the false lord fingered—the blaster with which he had once threatened Kincar. One of the slaves in his tail caught sight of the new party. His mouth opened on a scream of undisguised terror, and he flung himself to the floor, beating his fists against the stone pavement and continuing the yammering screech, which went on and on. His fellows cowered away, first from him, and then from their erstwhile leader as they saw the other Lord Dillan.

Even one with an iron will could not keep his attention from wandering at that interruption. The false lord glanced once to what lay behind him, giving those he held in check their chance. The Lady Asgar was at him in a fury, striving to wrest from him the blaster, while Kathal and Lord Jon's eldest son leaped to her support.

The rest of the party from the flier rushed in. Dillan, fresh stains of red seeping out on his bandaged shoulder, faced himself—but the likeness between them was no longer mirror-exact, for the Dillan of this Gorth snarled, his face awry in a grimace of rage. Asgar had torn the weapon from him. Now his bare hands reached for his rival's throat.

Kincar, as he had done to save Lord Bardon from the needle knife, clove through the distance between them, his left arm striking hard against the false lord's thighs, his sword tripping the other up. And they

219

smashed down on the pavement as others of the half-blood piled upon them.

When the false lord was safely pinned by Kathal and two of the others, Kincar sat up.

"Who are you?" demanded the prisoner of his standing double.

"I am the man you would have been had history in Gorth taken another path—"

The false Lord Dillan lay rigid; his mouth worked as if it were a struggle for him to force out the words. "But who—where—?"

"We found a path between parallel worlds—"

Dillan was alert to the Gorthians more than to his captive. Those of the ex-slaves who had followed the false lord were shrinking back. One or two whimpered. And the one who had howled and beat upon the floor was drooling as he stared vacantly at nothing. They were close to the breaking point.

It was the Lady Asgar who spoke to Kincar, drawing him to his feet with both hands and the urgency of her orders.

"This is a task for you, guardian. Give them something—a sign—they can fix upon. Or they may all lose their wits before our eyes!"

He tore open the sealing of his silver tunic and brought out the Tie. On his palm it emitted that soft glow of awakened power. And he began to chant, watching the glow brighten. Those of the half-blood took up his words. The sonorous sound filled the high vault of the hall. The stone warmed in his hold. He held it out to the Lady Asgar, and her larger hand cupped over it, sheltering the talisman with her alien flesh for a space as long as the chant of a line. There was no alteration in that glow, no harm to her.

Kincar turned to the Lord Dillan of the hold. In turn, that man's hand, broader, darker, arched without hesitation over the stone. Once more one of the Star blood passed that test.

Last of all the guardian stooped to the false lord. That Dillan, too, was not lacking in courage. His mouth set in a mirthless smile as the hand Kathal freed reached for the stone.

But in spite of his courage, his determination, he could not cup the Tie. It flared, pulsing not blue-green but a malignant yellow, as if some strange fire sent a tongue out of it at the encroaching hand.

"Demon!"

A bow cord sang, and a feathered shaft stood from a broad chest. The man on the floor arched his back and coughed, tried to fling some last word at his double. It was Kapal, clasping his bow to him, who laughed.

"One demon the less," he spat. "I care not if all his fellows be on the trail behind him. There is one demon less!"

"There will be none to follow him." The live Dillan spoke above the dead. "They have returned to the stars from which they came. Only this one broke from the ship just before it blasted—taking a flier. Gorth is now free of his breed."

From somewhere words flooded into Kincar's mind, began to pour from his tongue in a wild rhythm. He knew he had never learned them by rote, and together they formed a fearsome thing, a curse laid upon men in this world and the Forest beyond, upon their coming and going, their living and dying. The very beat of those words upon the air invoked strange shadows, and as he uttered them the ex-slaves crept about his feet, drinking them in.

Then from curse the words turned to promise, a promise such as the Three sometimes set in the mouths of those inspired by their wisdom.

"Lord—" It was Kapal who broke the silence that

221

fell when he ended. "What is your will for us?"

"Not my will." Kincar shook his head. "Do you live like free men in an open land—" But that fey streak still possessed him. He had one more thing that he must do. The Tie was dead now, a lifeless stone. For him it would never again grow warm or live. His guardianship was at an end. It must pass to another, perhaps one better fitted to use it as it should be used. He was but a messenger, not a true wielder of the Threefold Power.

"I show you a man of your own to lead you—" He turned slowly to face that other who was also s'Rud.

Kathal's hands came up slowly, as if they moved by some will outside his own. Kincar tossed the talisman into the air. It flashed straight across the space between them into those waiting hands. And as the stone touched flesh once more, it glowed! He had been right— the Tie had chosen to go from him. He could not, if he wished, take it again.

A faint promise of the coming warm season mellowed the stone at his back. Kincar breathed the fresh air from the courtyard. Vorken squatted on his shoulder, chirruping now and again.

"Stay with us, Lords—we need you—"

They had heard that plea repeated so many times during the past months. And, as ever, the same patient answer came.

"Not so. Us you need least of all. This is your world, Kathal, Kapal; shape your own roads through it. We did not sweep away one set of alien rulers to plant another. Take your fortune in your two hands and be glad it is truly yours!"

"But—where do you go, Lords? To a better world?"

Out in the valley was the shimmer of the now complete gate, erected from materials looted from the vanished ships. Did they seek a better world through that portal when on the morrow they went into a second self-imposed exile? Kincar reached for his bow. Would they ever find a Gorth to fit their dreams? Or did that greatly matter? Sometimes he thought that an endless quest had been set them for some purpose, and that the seeking, not the finding, was their full reward. And it was good.

ABOUT THE AUTHOR

Andre Norton is an outstanding science fiction/fantasy writer who is best known for the strange, memorable, wholly believable worlds she creates.

She has received the coveted Gandalf and Balrog Awards, and her works have been translated throughout the world.

She lives in Florida.